OTHER BOOKS BY JAE

Departure FROM the SCRIPT

JAE

ACKNOWLEDGMENTS

As with any creative project, there were a lot of people who had a hand in bringing this novella into existence, mainly Erin and Astrid, who kicked my butt when I wanted to end the story after the first kiss, and my critique partners, Alison Grey and RJ Nolan, who helped me revise with their invaluable feedback.

I also want to thank my test readers Betty, Henriette, and Michele for their time and their constructive criticism.

A big thank-you goes to Nikki Busch, editor extraordinaire, for her thorough yet fast work.

I'm more grateful for their help than I could ever express. Thanks!

AUTHOR'S NOTE

Departure from the Script started out as a short story, which has been published under the title "The Morning After," but Amanda and Michelle demanded more attention, so I extended it into a novella. At 52,000 words, some would even call it a novel.

Whatever you call it, I hope you enjoy reading it as much as I did writing about these two!

CHAPTER 1

SOMEONE WOULD DIE BEFORE DESSERT. Amanda was sure of that. She just didn't know yet who it was going to be. Either she would die of boredom, or her date would collapse face-first into her smoked salmon mousse, with Amanda's fork piercing her carotid.

Oblivious to Amanda's murderous intentions, Val prattled on and on and on. "...and so my parents made a deal that my father would get to name their first child and my mother would get to name the second. Oh, and you know what's really neat?" She clapped her hands.

"No," Amanda said, drawing on her acting skills to appear at least halfway interested. "What?" She lifted a deep-fried coconut shrimp to her mouth to cover her yawn.

"Val is short for Valentine, so Valentine's Day has always been my lucky day. I knew as soon as I met you that we were meant to be together forever."

Amanda nearly inhaled the shrimp. She coughed until her face had surely turned crimson. With two big gulps, she emptied her wine glass and looked around for the waiter. If she wanted to make it through this date, she needed some liquid encouragement. "Meant to be? Um, Val, this is our first date. Don't you think that's a little rushed, even for two lesbians?"

"Oh, not at all." Val reached across the table and ran one scarlet-painted nail down Amanda's arm. "True love doesn't know time."

Goose bumps followed in the wake of Val's touch. Too bad they weren't the pleasant type. Under the pretense of emptying her glass, which the waiter had just refilled, Amanda pulled her arm away. *All right. I'm out of here.*

Before she could think of a polite way to escape this date from hell, the waiter interrupted. He set down the wild-mushroom pasta in front of her and then walked around the table to serve Val's ricotta ravioli.

Still jabbering nonstop, Val reached for her fork and used it to cut her ravioli into little heart-shaped pieces.

Amanda stared at Val's plate. *Oh God, she's a love psycho.* She felt as if she were stuck in one of the badly written daily soaps she had auditioned for, but there was no one yelling, "cut" when things weren't going well.

"You'll love my parents," Val said. "I know they'll fall in love with you at first sight too, just like I did. Maybe we could drive up and visit them next weekend. They live in Carmel. It's a nice drive, very romantic." She made googly eyes at Amanda.

In a second, she would probably start playing footsie under the table.

Amanda craned her neck, searching for the nearest exit.

"Damn." Val dabbed frantically at a bit of tomato sauce that had splashed onto her blouse. She rubbed and scrubbed but only succeeded in making it worse. Her chair scraped across the floor as she jumped up. "Would you excuse me for a moment? I need to…" She waved at her chest and hurried away.

Yes! Amanda stood too. This was her chance to beat a hasty retreat. But was it really fair to put enough money on the table to pay for her half of dinner and leave? She threw a longing glance at the exit but then sighed and sat back down. Too bad her grandmother had raised her better than that. Val might be nuttier than a fruitcake, but Amanda didn't want to spoil her lucky day forever by leaving her in the middle of their date without any explanation.

Cursing herself, she fumbled to retrieve her cell phone from her purse and pressed number two on the speed dial.

The phone rang twice before it was picked up. "Hi," Kathryn said. "What can I do for my favorite client?"

"You can promise to never, ever set me up on a blind date again."

"Oh." Kathryn paused. "I take it your date isn't going well? Rob swore on his brother's grave that she's exactly the type of woman you go for."

Amanda snorted. "Rob's an only child."

Paper rustled on the other end of the line. "So Val isn't your type?"

Hell no, Amanda wanted to shout, but she forced herself to be fair. "When I first saw her, I thought she was." Truth be told, Val was exactly her type—at least in the looks department: Her wavy, red hair fell in stylish curls past her slender shoulders. She was dressed in an elegant blouse and a black miniskirt that was sexy yet tasteful. And she moved with more grace than many of Amanda's fellow actresses.

"And then?" Kathryn asked. "What happened?"

"She opened her mouth." Amanda took another sip of red wine.

"Oh, come on. Don't be such a snob. She can't be that bad."

"Oh, no? How would you like a date that tells you her entire life story—and that of every member of her family—before you can even order dinner? And then she proceeds to plan your future together because she's convinced you're meant for each other." Amanda emptied her glass and shook herself. "I bet by the time we order dessert, she'll have our children's lives all mapped out."

Kathryn laughed. "You're not kidding, are you?"

"I wish I were." Amanda raised her hand to summon the waiter. After he refilled her glass, she nodded her thanks.

"Where is your date from hell?" Kathryn asked. "Have you fled to the bathroom?"

"No, she did. She dropped a bit of her heart-shaped ravioli on her blouse." Amanda kept one eye on the door to the ladies' room. Val could be back any minute. "Kath, you have to help me. I need to get out of here before she drops to one knee and proposes in the middle of the restaurant."

Kathryn's muffled giggle reverberated through the phone. "Just tell her Steven Spielberg called and wants you for his next movie, so you need to leave right away to meet with him."

"Spielberg." Amanda snorted. "Sure, she'll believe that. He saw me in the last commercial I did and was so blown away by the finesse I used when holding up that dishwashing liquid that he wants to hire me on the spot."

"Stranger things have happened," Kathryn said.

"Not to me."

The door to the ladies' room opened.

Amanda's heartbeat tripled.

An elderly woman stepped back into the restaurant.

Amanda blew out a breath. "The strangest thing that happened to me is this date. This is like the dating *Twilight Zone*."

"Can't be worse than the first date with my second husband," Kathryn said. "He—"

"Kath, I'd love to listen to your story, but I only have a few seconds before Val is back. Help!"

"Okay, okay. I'll think of something and call you back." Kathryn ended the call.

Moments after Amanda put the cell phone away, Val left the ladies' room and returned to the table. She had clearly tried to remove the stain with water and soap from the bathroom sink, so now her wet blouse was nearly see-through and stuck to her well-endowed chest.

Down, girl, Amanda told her libido. *This woman's like cotton candy. She might look tasty, but she's bad for you...and sticky as hell.*

Val took a seat and picked up her fork again. Within less than a minute, she had made half a dozen more ravioli hearts. "Sorry about that. So tell me a bit about yourself," she said. "What did you think when you first met me?"

A piece of mushroom nearly lodged in Amanda's windpipe. *I think I'll be the one to die tonight. Asphyxiation, most likely.* She took another sip of red wine. *Or maybe cirrhosis of the liver.*

Her cell phone rang to the tones of Madonna's "Hollywood."

Saved by the bell. "Oh, excuse me. I have to take this call. It's my agent." Amanda broke a speed record when she reached for her cell phone.

"Oh, Amanda, I'm so glad you're home," Kathryn whimpered into the phone with the fake despair of a wannabe actress.

"Um, you called my cell. I'm not home." Amanda peeked across the table.

Val was watching her expectantly as if she thought her agent had called with an offer from Hollywood.

Damn. Maybe we should have tried that Spielberg excuse. "What's wrong?" Amanda asked, adding just a hint of concern to her tone.

Kathryn was less subtle. Crying sounds echoed through the phone, probably loud enough that Val could hear them. "My husband just filed for a divorce."

Which one? Amanda nearly asked. Kath had been divorced three times and was currently as single as Amanda. "Oh my God! Sweetie, I'm so sorry. That's just awful. What an asshole." She smashed her fist onto the table. Her wine glass wobbled, and she made a quick grab to prevent it from toppling over. "Just wait until I get my hands on that cheating, lying bastard!"

The crying turned into heaving sobs.

"Don't cry. I'll come over and either kill him or make him change his mind."

Kathryn blew her nose. It sounded like an elephant. "You'd do that for me?"

"Of course. I'll be there as soon as I can." Amanda ended the call and slid her cell phone back into her purse.

When she glanced up, Val was staring at her. Her lipstick-red lips formed a pout. "You have to leave?"

"Yes. I'm really sorry. It was a wonderful evening, and I'm sorry to see it end." *Wow, I deserve an Oscar for managing to say that with a straight face.* "But my agent really needs me tonight. Her husband just filed for divorce."

"Oh my God! On Valentine's Day?" Val pressed both hands to her damp chest. "Believe me, I would never do something like that to you."

Yeah, that's for sure. Because I won't let it come to that. Amanda forced a smile, laid a few bills on the table, and got up.

Val jumped up. "Do you want me to come with you? I could—"

"Oh, no, no," Amanda said so fast that she nearly tied her tongue in knots. "You stay and enjoy the rest of your dinner. I'm sure Kathryn would hate for anyone else to see her like that."

Slowly, Val sank back onto her chair. "You could come over to my place once you're finished with your agent."

Sweat broke out along Amanda's back. *Christ. How do I get out of this one?* "I can't," she said. "I'll probably stay over at Kathryn's. She shouldn't be alone tonight."

"You're so thoughtful." If Val had been a comic character, her gaze would have sent little pink hearts in Amanda's direction.

"Um, yeah. That's me." Before Val could ask for a second date, Amanda waved and hurried out of the restaurant.

Amanda leaned against the driver's side of her car and exhaled slowly, feeling as if she had just narrowly escaped death. She reached for her cell phone and again pressed number two on her speed dial.

"Did you make it out of the *Twilight Zone*?" Kathryn asked without even saying *hi*.

"Yeah. Thank God." Amanda dabbed her brow. "And by the way, your acting is abysmal."

Kathryn snorted. "What do you expect? There's a reason why I'm the agent and you're the actress."

"Yes, because being an agent pays better," Amanda said.

"There's that too."

Amanda fished her car keys out of her purse. "If you see Rob, tell him he owes me—big."

"Will do. Oh, and Amanda? Happy Valentine's Day." Kathryn hung up before Amanda could answer.

Shaking her head, Amanda put away her cell phone. When she reached out to unlock the door, her gaze fell on a flyer tucked under the windshield wiper. She reached around and pulled it free.

The little red hearts dotting the flyer made her tighten her fingers, about to crumple it up. She had enough of romance for today. But at the last moment, a picture of Cupid caught her attention. Instead of shooting arrows at potential lovers, he lay facedown on a bloodstained floor. An arrow pierced his back right between his little white wings. Below the picture, bilious green letters announced, "Anti-Valentine's Day party."

Amanda laughed and continued to read, "Are you sick of mushy cards, cheap chocolate, and the pressure of finding a date?" Her head bobbed up and down as she nodded vigorously. "God, yes!" That party didn't sound so bad after all. She threw a glance at her wristwatch.

Just after nine.

According to the flyer, the Anti-Valentine's Day party had started at eight. And it was right around the corner.

She hefted the keys in her hand and then put them back into her purse.

After her date, she could use the company of a few people not looking for love, especially if the crowd was mostly straight people. She'd had enough of women searching for their soul mate. One drink, then she'd call a taxi and go home. After having two or three glasses of wine with dinner, she shouldn't drive anyway.

Decision made, she crossed the street, whistling "No More I Love You's."

Amanda slid onto the last empty stool at the bar and turned to let her gaze wander through the club.

Broken hearts, black roses, and posters of the movie *The War of the Roses* decorated the walls. A mixed crowd of men and women, mostly in their twenties and thirties, danced to "This Is Not a Love Song." Amanda realized that no one was wearing red or pink. Instead, some of the guests wore T-shirts that said "Love stinks," "Happy to be single," or "Cupid is stupid."

Someone cleared his throat behind her.

Amanda turned.

The bartender, a guy with tattoos on nearly every visible inch of skin, gave her a nod. "What'll it be?"

Eyeing the cocktail menu behind the bar, she rubbed her chin. The menu listed drinks with names such as "one-night stand," "breakup," and "free love," along with some more traditional choices. She wasn't much of a liquor drinker. Usually, she stuck to red wine. But after a day like this, she could use something stronger. "Any suggestions?"

"How about a 'witchy woman'?" the bartender asked. "That's a mix of Campari, rum, orange juice, and lime juice."

"Witchy woman? No, thanks," Amanda mumbled. "I've had enough of that for one evening."

"Pardon me?"

"I said it's too sour for me. How about something sweet?"

A barrel-chested guy in an "It's not me; it's you" T-shirt sauntered over to the bar and squeezed in between Amanda and the woman on the bar stool to her right. "I think the lady needs a 'southern screw,'" he drawled in a fake southern accent.

The bartender looked at Amanda, his hands hovering over the shaker.

Amanda turned to face the barrel-chested guy. With his red hair and pearly-white smile, he could have been Val's brother. "That's a very lame pick-up line, even for an Anti-Valentine's Day party."

He shrugged. "You could teach me a better one."

His grin wouldn't have worked on her even if she were straight. "No, thanks." She was an actress, not a stage prompter for romantically challenged guys. Turning back to the bartender, she said, "Now I need something strong."

"Whatever she wants, it's on me," the redhead said.

Ignoring him, Amanda laid a ten-dollar bill on the bar.

The bartender took the money and shoveled ice cubes into a glass. "How about a mix of vodka, coffee liqueur, and tonic water? It's called 'mind eraser.'"

She hadn't drunk vodka for years, but for some reason, it seemed like the right thing to end a day like this, so she shrugged. "Why not?"

As the alcohol burned down her throat, making her cough, the thought *Famous last words* ran through her mind, but then the red-haired man told the bartender to keep the drinks coming and she forgot everything else.

CHAPTER 2

WHOEVER HAD SAID VODKA DIDN'T induce a hangover was a goddamn liar. Amanda's head pounded like a bass drum being beaten by a hyperactive preschooler. Groaning, she pressed her hands to her temples, but the movement only made it worse. Her stomach roiled like a washing machine with a turbo spin cycle, and she lay perfectly still until the wave of nausea ebbed away.

Oh God, she wanted to say, but her tongue was glued to the roof of her mouth. She smacked her lips and grimaced. Her mouth tasted as if she'd been licking the inside of a rubber boot.

Blindly, she reached out one hand for the water bottle she kept on her nightstand.

It wasn't there.

Neither was the nightstand.

What the...? Was she caught in some alcohol-induced nightmare, like the one in which she had won an Oscar, but when she wanted to walk onto the stage to accept it, she couldn't find her clothes? She opened her eyes.

Sunlight made her wince. The crazed preschooler was now stomping on her head.

She squeezed her eyes shut and pulled the pillow over her head to shut out the sunlight. The smell of men's cologne clung to the cotton pillow cover.

Nonsense. How much of that hellish stuff had she drunk last night? Now not even her sense of smell was working. There was no way men's cologne could cling to her pillow. Her bed was a man-free zone.

Wait a minute… Cotton? Just a few days ago, she had put the satin sheets that Kathryn had given her for Christmas on her bed.

She jerked upright and then clutched her head. Through half-open eyes, she peered at the unfamiliar bedroom. To her left was a floor-to-ceiling window. Her head spun as she stared at a stone patio surrounded by lemon and orange trees, so different from the view that greeted her when she opened her eyes in her modest one-bedroom apartment.

Large black-and-white prints covered the rest of the walls—a Harley with a half-naked woman straddling the bike, a close-up of a growling tiger, and the weathered face of an old man squinting into the sun.

A man's wristwatch sat on the nightstand on the other side of the bed. Next to it, clothes were piled on a white leather-and-chrome chair: socks, a pair of boxer shorts, and a Los Angeles Lakers sweatshirt. A pair of sneakers that looked to be at least a size ten lay beneath the chair.

Amanda glanced back and forth between the Harley print, the watch, and the boxer shorts. Her nose caught another whiff of men's cologne. *Oh, shit. What did I do? No way in hell did I go home with that guy from the bar…did I?*

Not even half a dozen of those mind erasers could turn a gay woman straight. *Stupid maybe, but not straight.*

Her gaze darted down her body. Air whooshed out of her lungs. *Thank God.* At least she was still wearing her panties and bra. She massaged her hammering temples, hoping it would jog her memory of what had happened last night.

No such luck. The last thing she remembered was drinking at the bar and pulling her blouse down from her shoulder to show off the scar from that commercial with the camel.

Her red-haired drinking companion had clapped and hooted.

Everything after that was a blank.

God, I hate Valentine's Day. And mind erasers. And if I slept with a man, I really, really hate myself. Even as a teenager, she had known that her interests lay elsewhere, and she had never succumbed to Hollywood's pressure to date men. She had always been proud of that, but now...

When the pounding in her head lessened for a moment, she became aware of the sound of a running shower. Someone whistled a much-too-happy tune in the bathroom.

Amanda's stomach lurched. She didn't want to even imagine what had put the guy in this postcoital mood.

The water stopped. He would be out in a minute.

Time to make a quick escape. Ignoring the drumroll in her head, Amanda jumped up. Her feet got caught in something soft, and she nearly fell. Suppressing a curse, she looked down.

Her slacks, blouse, and socks were strewn around the bed as if ripped off in the heat of passion. When she bent down and picked up her clothes, the world started spinning. She waited until the merry-go-round stopped before she shoved first one foot, then the other through a pant leg and struggled to pull up her slacks.

A sound made her look up, half in, half out of her pants.

Clouds of steam drifted through the now-open bathroom door.

Amanda froze and took in the figure in the doorway. She wanted to squeeze her eyes shut but forced her gaze to trail up muscular legs clad in worn jeans and over a black muscle shirt clinging to still-damp skin. Next, she encountered—

Breasts! They weren't overly large, but that definitely wasn't the chest of the red-haired guy or any other man. Only her pounding head and the slacks trapping her feet prevented her from doing a dance of joy. *I knew it! I would never sleep with...* Her gaze wandered farther and took in short hair and a strong face. *A butch?*

She had never dated, much less slept with, a butch.

With her feet still tangled in her slacks, she fell backward.

The bed broke her fall, and she lay still, staring at the ceiling.

Concerned brown eyes appeared in her line of sight. "You okay, Mandy?"

"Mandy?" Amanda croaked. Only her grandmother was allowed to call her that.

One knee next to Amanda on the bed, much too close for her liking, the butch looked down at her. "Yeah. Last night, you told me to call you Mandy."

Dear God. What else had she done last night? She didn't dare ask.

"Something wrong with that?" the butch asked when Amanda stayed silent. "It's your name, isn't it?"

"Yes, it is. But…ah, you know, it doesn't matter. I have to go." She rolled to the side and got up, careful to avoid stumbling over her slacks again.

"Like this?" The butch moved away from the bed and gestured at Amanda's state of dress…or rather state of undress. "You're welcome to take a shower first, then I'll drive you back to your car."

So at least she hadn't gotten behind the wheel drunk last night. Not that getting into a car with a complete stranger was much better. Amanda hesitated, but the thought of a hot shower was tempting. "All right." She pulled up her slacks, picked up the blouse, and clutched it to her chest as she passed the woman on her way to the bathroom. *Like she hasn't seen it all already.*

"I put clean towels and a toothbrush out for you," the butch said. "Do you need something to wear?"

"Uh, no, thank you." Boxer shorts and muscle shirts really weren't her style. Yesterday's clothes would have to do until she made it home. Amanda quickly closed and locked the bathroom door behind her and sank onto the edge of the tub. She rubbed her face with both hands and moaned into her palms. When she pulled her hands away, her gaze fell on the mirror above the sink.

Her reflection looked as bad as she felt. Good thing she didn't have an acting job lined up today. Not even the world's best makeup artist could have covered the shadows beneath her eyes or the greenish tint of her skin. Her hair looked as if a bird—or an entire flock—had made a nest in it.

She gave herself a mental shove. *Hurry up before she thinks you're in here rooting through the bathroom cabinets or she breaks down the door to save you from drowning in the tub.* She slipped out of the still-unbuttoned slacks, kicked off her panties, and unhooked her bra before stepping into the shower. The hot water felt heavenly.

While she washed up, she took stock of her body. Other than the second-worst hangover of her life, everything seemed normal. No hickeys. No scratches on her back. No sensitive body parts. Nothing that indicated a night of passionate, intense sex—and with the athletic butch, it probably would have been intense. *Maybe you weren't up for more than a quickie, as smashed as you were.*

She squeezed shampoo into her hand and sniffed at it. Instead of the honey and cream she was used to, her hostess's shampoo had a minty herbal scent. When she scrubbed her scalp, she flinched. Even the roots of her hair hurt.

As the soapy water ran down her back, an image flashed through her mind: the butch's muscular arms wrapped around her, pulling her against her warm, tight body. She buried her fingers in short, silky hair. When two insistent hands slid down her ass, she lifted her head and captured the butch's lips in a deep kiss.

Despite her killer headache, her body reacted to the memory. *Stop it. You've never been attracted to butch women. Vodka just makes you horny.* She shut off the water, stepped out of the shower, and struggled back into her clothes.

As promised, a toothbrush, still in its package, waited next to the sink.

Unlike Amanda, who avoided one-night stands, her hostess was obviously used to having overnight guests. But when she managed to get the toothbrush out of its package, she realized that it was smaller than usual. Tiny panda bears dotted the handle. *She gave me a toothbrush for children?*

She shrugged and squeezed toothpaste onto the pink-and-white-striped bristles, eager to get rid of that rubber-boot taste in her mouth. Finally feeling halfway human again, she stepped out of the bathroom and went in search of her hostess.

She padded over the hardwood floor and took in the house. The hall opened into a large living area, and Amanda couldn't help staring as she took in the view of the Hollywood Hills beyond the French doors.

Well, at least she had taste—apparently, she had slept with someone rich and/or famous.

23

Two steps led from the living room up to the kitchen, which seemed to have every cooking gadget known to mankind.

"How many pancakes do you want?" the butch called from the stove.

What is it about lesbians and their instant domesticity? Had she stumbled across a butch version of Val? Her stomach roiled at the mere thought of food. "No pancakes for me."

The butch turned and leaned against the counter. She was barefoot, and her dark brown hair was tousled and still damp from her shower. Amanda usually preferred women in skirts to women in jeans, but even she had to admit that her hostess had a sexy ass.

"Are you sure? I haven't poisoned anyone yet, if that's what you're worried about." The butch turned back to the stove. With a quick flick of her wrist, she flipped the pancake. It landed back in the pan without a splash.

Amanda lifted a brow. Most butches she knew were helpless in the kitchen. Not that she knew many.

"You'll feel better once you have something in your stomach. Let me make you some toast. Or do you want oatmeal?"

"No, no. That's not necessary. I can eat when I get home."

The butch turned off the stove and swiveled to face Amanda. Her biceps flexed as she crossed her arms over her chest. "It's Saturday. You've got somewhere urgent to be?"

Amanda glanced at her watch. It was barely eight, so she had more than seven hours before her shift at the juice bar started. "Um, no, but…"

"But…?"

What could she say? *No, thanks, I'm not in the habit of letting people make me breakfast when I don't even know their name?* She sighed. After spending the night with this stranger, the least she could do was accept her hospitality and have breakfast with her. "All right. Then I'll have toast if it's not too much trouble."

"No trouble at all." The butch moved smoothly through the modern chef's kitchen and popped two pieces of bread into the toaster. "Come over here and sit down. I don't bite."

Amanda flushed. What was she? A fifteen-year-old? Women usually didn't fluster her like this. She climbed the two steps to the kitchen and sat at the far side of the breakfast bar, careful not to get in the butch's way. When the toaster ejected the toast, Amanda jumped and then scolded herself.

The butch placed two perfect, golden-brown pieces of toast in front of her. "Butter?"

"Um, no, thanks." Amanda wasn't even sure her stomach could handle the toast.

After one long glance at Amanda, the woman put a kettle of water on the stove.

While they waited for the water to boil, the silence seemed deafening. Amanda fidgeted, but even if she had been in the mood for a chat, she didn't know what to say.

A few minutes later, the butch set a steaming mug down in front of her.

"Thank you." Amanda took a careful sniff. The fresh, spicy scent reminded her of her favorite Chinese takeout. "What's this?"

A smile deepened the laugh lines around the butch's eyes. She couldn't be much older than Amanda's thirty-one, but the lines in her face already showed that she liked to laugh. "Don't worry. I told you I'm not gonna poison you. It's fresh ginger tea. My grandfather always made it for me when I felt a bit…under the weather."

Under the weather. Amanda couldn't help returning the smile. That's what her grandmother also called it when someone had a hangover. She clutched the mug in both hands and let the warmth soothe her rattled nerves.

The butch pulled up a stool, took a seat next to her at the breakfast bar, and got started on her stack of pancakes. Her knee touched Amanda's, but she either didn't notice or was entirely comfortable sitting so close.

No wonder. She touched a lot more than just your knee last night and probably remembers every last graphic detail. Amanda didn't, though. To her, the woman was a complete stranger. Under the pretense of reaching for her toast, she pulled her knee away.

In the silence between them, the crunching of the toast sounded overly loud. Should she say something? But what? As far as she could see, they had nothing in common. Finally, she thought of something. "You've got kids?"

The butch swallowed a bite of pancake and looked up. "Oh, you mean because of the toothbrush? Sorry about that. It was the only new one I had. I keep some for when my nieces and nephews stay overnight. I don't have kids, but I'm a highly sought-after babysitter."

"Oh." Somehow, she hadn't thought of the butch as the babysitter type. Amanda rolled her eyes at herself. *Stereotyping much?*

"You sound surprised. Butch women can be great with kids too. We also have a fully functional uterus, you know?" She didn't sound offended, just amused.

Amanda's cheeks heated. She hid behind the mug of tea. "I know. It's just... This...you... It just caught me off-guard." Oh, great. If her acting coach had heard her, he would have lost what little hair he had left. Years of voice training and now one night with this stranger made her stammer like a fool. "I don't usually... You're not... I mean, normally, I go for the more..."

"Feminine type," the butch said with a nod. "I know. That's what you said last night."

"Oh. I did?" *Was that before or after I examined her tonsils with my tongue?*

The butch put down her fork and turned to face Amanda. "You don't remember a thing about last night, do you?"

Amanda nearly spat ginger tea across the breakfast bar. Her coughing made the hyperactive preschooler start the drumming behind her temples again. Wheezing, she peeked at the butch out of the corner of her eye. What now? Lie through her teeth or come clean? She decided to go with the truth. Sort of. "Everything after the first drink is a bit fuzzy."

The butch lifted one perfectly arched eyebrow.

Was she tweezing them, or did they naturally grow like that?

"Define 'a bit fuzzy.'"

"Um." Amanda nibbled on her toast to buy herself some time. Finally, she wiped the crumbs off her chin and turned toward the woman next to her. "I don't remember a thing." There. It was out. She gulped down ginger tea as if it were liquor.

"Nothing? Not even...?"

"What?" Amanda asked. "What happened?"

The butch shook her head. "Nothing."

Amanda wanted to believe that, but she remembered a pretty hot kiss. Maybe the butch thought nothing of kissing strangers on a regular basis, but in Amanda's book, that wasn't "nothing."

"Honestly. We didn't sleep together." The butch looked at her with her brown teddy bear eyes. Either she was a damn good liar or a better actress than Amanda.

"But you kissed me."

"No."

The half-empty mug nearly toppled over as Amanda stabbed her finger at the butch. "Liar. That's the one thing I remember. You kissed me, and it wasn't a little peck."

"No," the butch said once more. "You kissed me."

"Why would I do that?" Only after she had said it did Amanda realize how that sounded. Christ. She was acting as if the butch was the most repulsive creature on earth, and that certainly wasn't true. "Sorry. That didn't come out the way I meant it. What I meant is, uh…"

"That red-haired guy just wouldn't leave you alone, no matter how many times you told him to clear out. After you shot him down for the umpteenth time, he slurred, 'What are you, a lesbian?' By that time, half of the club was eavesdropping on your conversation."

Amanda groaned. As much as she appreciated having an attentive audience at work, she hated making a spectacle of herself in her spare time.

"You looked him right in the eye and said, 'Yes.'" The butch shrugged. "That idiot didn't believe you, so you set out to convince him."

Something tickled the edges of Amanda's memory. Not quite a flashback, but the words rang true. "What did I do?" She had a feeling she wouldn't like the answer.

"You emptied your drink, turned, and laid the kiss of my life on me." Grinning, the butch fanned herself with both hands.

"I didn't."

"You sure did. And it was very convincing too. After he stopped salivating, the guy finally got lost."

Amanda covered her burning face with her hands. "Oh my God. I'm so sorry."

Gentle fingers tried to pull her hands down, but she resisted. "No need to apologize. Even three sheets to the wind, you're a great kisser."

Still feeling as if her face was glowing ketchup red, Amanda peeked through her fingers. For the first time, she really looked at the butch's face. Despite the short hair, it wasn't as androgynous as she had first thought. The square jaw and strong forehead were gentled by luscious lips and long eyelashes that every actress in Hollywood, including Amanda, would kill for. A small scar at the corner of her left eye made her look as if she were constantly winking. Somehow, it seemed to fit her easygoing personality.

The woman gave her an encouraging smile.

Amanda took her hands away from her face and inhaled deeply, determined to be an adult about this. "Okay. So I kissed you, and you didn't suffer too much. That still doesn't explain how I ended up in your bed." She tried to keep her voice neutral, without an accusing undertone. The woman next to her didn't seem like the type who took advantage of a drunken person.

"People were staring at you, so I dragged you out of that bar before you could order another one of those drinks."

"I wish you'd had that idea before I drank enough to put down a rhino," Amanda mumbled and rubbed her temples.

An impish grin flashed across the butch's face. "Sorry."

"What happened then?"

"I offered to drive you home or call you a taxi, but you refused to tell me where you live. Now I'm not so sure you even remembered your address. So it was either let you wander about the parking lot in the middle of the night or take you home with me."

That sounded plausible. Amanda wasn't proud of drinking so much that she lost her memory and all sense of orientation, but at least she hadn't slept with a complete stranger. "And why didn't I sleep in the guestroom?" From what she had seen of the house, it was big enough to have at least a second bedroom.

"I don't have one. I turned the second bedroom into a studio when I first moved in."

So her rescuer was an artist. Or was she talking about a recording studio? Amanda shook her still pounding head and curbed her curiosity. They'd never see each other again, so it didn't matter what she did for a living. "Then why didn't I sleep on the couch?"

"Because that's where I slept," the butch said. "My grandfather would turn in his grave if I let a lady sleep on the couch."

Amanda sighed. "I didn't behave like much of a lady last night."

The butch chuckled. "Um, no, you didn't. Your wandering hands almost landed us in the ditch twice before we finally made it to my house."

"Excuse me?" Amanda squinted at the woman. She was kidding, right? With her constant wink, Amanda couldn't tell.

"You really, really seemed to like my thighs and…um… well, a few other body parts."

31

Amanda wanted to sink under the breakfast bar and never come out again. Out of the corner of her eye, she peeked at the butch's thighs. Even though she liked her women not quite so athletic, she had to admit that this was a fine pair of legs. *Cut it out!* She jerked her gaze upward. What the hell was going on with her? Never, ever in her life would she drink those mind erasers again. That drink was really messing with her head, even now, on the morning after. "But when we got here, I behaved myself, right?"

"Ah, well, you tried to undress me, but... Don't get me wrong, if we had met under different circumstances, I certainly wouldn't push you out of bed," the butch flashed a grin that showed off even, white teeth, "but sleeping with a drunken woman is not my style. I just led you to my bedroom, where you struggled out of your clothes, fell face-first on my bed, and started snoring like a lumberjack."

Okay, it's official now. I'll be the one to die—of embarrassment. Amanda sent her a pleading gaze. "I'm really, really sorry."

"Again, you've got nothing to apologize for. Well, the snoring wasn't half as pleasant as the kissing, but it was kind of cute." The butch chuckled.

Amanda made a face. "No, really. You went to a lot of trouble to get me out of a bad situation, and all I do when I wake up is treat you as if you did something wrong."

"It's okay. I'd freak out too if I woke up in a stranger's house, not knowing what happened."

For a few minutes, they sat next to each other without talking, Amanda busy digesting what she'd just found out and the butch eating her pancakes, which had probably gone cold by now.

"So," the butch said when she carried the dishes to the sink, "anything else you want to know about last night?"

"I've got one more question," Amanda said. "But it's not about last night."

"Oh? What is it, then? Come on, out with it." The butch turned and winked with her right eye, the one that didn't have the scar. "After doing the tonsil tango with me, there's no reason to be shy."

Ignoring her blush, Amanda finally asked, "What's your name?" She still didn't know this stranger, but thinking of her just as "the butch" didn't feel right anymore.

The woman chuckled. She piled the dishes in the sink, wiped her fingers on her jeans, and held out her right hand. "Michelle Osinski. Nice to meet you."

"Amanda Clark." She shook Michelle's hand. "And what do you go by?"

Michelle's brows pinched together. "Go by?" Then her expression cleared. "Oh, you thought... No, it's just Michelle."

"Oh. Okay." For some reason, Amanda had expected a more tough-sounding nickname. *One more stereotype bites the dust.*

Michelle laughed. "You thought all butches have names like Chris, Mel, or Sam? Sorry to disappoint."

"Um, no, of course I didn't think that." Amanda rubbed her cheeks. They were burning, as were her earlobes.

Michelle patted her arm. "Relax, will you? I'm just teasing." She put her hands in her jeans pockets.

Amanda couldn't help watching the muscles play in her arms. Normally, she didn't like buff women, but on Michelle, it looked natural. She wrenched her gaze away and rubbed her eyes. *I'll never drink vodka again. Ever.*

"Now that you've got something in your stomach, I'll get you a Tylenol," Michelle said. "Let's go get comfortable while we wait for the painkillers to kick in." She put her hand on the small of Amanda's back as if she wanted to lead her to the living room.

Her touch made Amanda's skin heat up. Uncomfortable with her body's strange reaction, she pulled away. "No, thanks. My headache is a lot better already." She was ready to escape this embarrassing situation and go home.

After studying Amanda more intently than most casting directors, Michelle shook her head and said, "You really don't like me, do you?"

"W-what?" Amanda stood and white-knuckled the edge of the breakfast bar. "What makes you think that?" Had she really given Michelle that impression? If anything, she was grateful for her help. Grateful and mortally embarrassed.

"You keep looking at me like you're afraid I'm going to try and lure you back into bed and have my way with you."

"No, that's not—"

"Listen, I got the message. You don't go for butch women. And that's fine with me because I," Michelle tapped her chest, "promised myself to never, ever get involved with an actress again. Two of my exes are actresses, and no offense,

34

but I could do without the drama that comes with being in a relationship with a Hollywood diva."

Wow. Amanda sank against the breakfast bar. "Are you always so direct?" In her world full of flatterers, opportunists, and professional pretenders, no one ever came right out and told her what he or she thought of her. Well, no one but the camel that let her know in no uncertain terms that it didn't like her—by biting her.

"Usually," Michelle said, shrugging. "It saves time." With a rueful smile she added, "It also got me slapped a time or two."

Her expression made Amanda laugh. "Your actress exes?"

"No. Throwing dishes was more their style."

Oh, yeah. Amanda had once shared a trailer with a soap opera diva like that. "Is that how you got your scar?" She pointed at the corner of her eye and then jerked her hand away. She normally wasn't one to ask such personal questions the first time she met someone. *Guess being direct is contagious.*

Automatically, Michelle's finger came up to touch the scar. "No. I got quite good at ducking the occasional flying plate. I had that scar long before I met my exes. But the story of how I got it is not quite as spectacular as what happened with your scar."

Amanda groaned. "Did the whole bar see my shoulder?"

"No, not the whole bar. I was sitting right next to you when you showed off that scar."

Even now, Amanda's memory remained blank. She hazily remembered sliding onto a barstool. Yes, a woman had been sitting next to her, but she hadn't paid her any attention. "Are you trying to change the topic? We were talking about your scar, not mine."

"Guilty as charged, ma'am." Michelle lifted both hands. "Okay, here's the story. When I was four or five, my brother and I were fighting over some toy. I tackled him, and when he tried to crawl away with the toy, I held on to his leg. That's when he kicked out."

"Ouch." For once, Amanda was glad to be an only child. "Who got the toy in the end?"

Michelle chuckled. "Who do you think?"

"I have a feeling you always get what you want."

A grin tugged up the small scar. "Does that mean you'll come to the living room with me?" Michelle sobered. "Listen, I'm really not trying to get fresh with you or anything, but you look like hell. You should really take a Tylenol and wait for it to kick in before you get behind the wheel."

Her honesty was disarming. And she was right. Driving with a hangover was almost as bad as drunk driving. Waiting a few more minutes before they left wouldn't hurt, especially now that they both knew where they stood. "All right. You win."

Michelle's living room made Amanda's small apartment seem like an emergency shelter. Two recliners were angled toward a cozy fireplace that made the stylish room look more inviting. A red fleece blanket had slipped off the leather couch, where Michelle had slept.

As in the bedroom, framed prints dominated this room too. Next to the TV hung a large photograph of two gnarled, age-spotted hands cradling a tiny baby. In another print, half a dozen kids between the ages of two and twelve piled onto Michelle, hugging her. All of them shared the same hair and eye color, like rich Swiss chocolate. Michelle, who was crouched to be at eye level with the smaller kids, looked as if she was about to be toppled under the onslaught, but instead of catching herself, she steadied the youngest child with both hands, preventing him from falling.

"That's a great picture," Amanda said, pointing.

Michelle turned and regarded the photo with a fond expression. "Yeah. That's my brother's brood."

Amanda stared at her. "Your brother has six children?"

"What can I say? Marty never knew when to stop." Michelle set the bottle of painkillers and a glass of water on the coffee table. She bent, picked up the blanket, and folded it. Sweeping her arm, she invited Amanda to sit.

Amanda took two steps toward her and then stopped when the largest DVD collection she had ever seen caught her attention; even her own paled in comparison. There had to be at least one thousand DVDs, filling shelf after shelf in a ceiling-high bookcase. "Wow. Apparently, you don't know when to stop either."

Michelle laughed. Not the polite little laugh or dainty giggle that was so common in Hollywood circles, but a full-out laugh that seemed to fill the air with joy.

At the loud sound, Amanda's headache flared up, making her wince.

"Sorry." Michelle stopped laughing and pressed her fingers to her full lips, but her eyes still twinkled. "Yeah, I go a bit overboard when it comes to movies. Would I have anything that you're in?"

Amanda had long since learned to expect that question whenever people found out she was an actress. "Do you tape commercials or bad soap operas?"

"Um, no."

"Then no, you don't have anything I'm in."

An understanding smile spread across Michelle's face. "Ah, so your career hasn't yet taken off. Don't worry; it will. You've got the face for it."

Amanda eyed her. Was Michelle one of these smooth-talking butches who complimented women left and right? After almost five years in Hollywood, Amanda was immune to that kind of flattery. "Thanks, I think," she said and crossed the room. "At least your lines are much better than those of my red-haired drinking buddy." She winced as soon as she had said it. Being hungover sure didn't improve her tactfulness.

"Lines?" Michelle shook her head. "Nope. I leave delivering lines to you actresses. I really meant it. You know, you remind me of my favorite actress of all time. I thought so as soon as I saw you last night."

"So who's your favorite actress? Sandra Bullock in *Twenty-Eight Days*?" Amanda couldn't remember most of last night, but her behavior must have been just as embarrassing as that of the movie's alcoholic main character. She took a step toward the coffee table to pick up the Tylenol.

Michelle laughed, though not as loudly as before. "No. It wasn't the fact that you were drinking like a fish that reminded me of my favorite actress. It's the way you move and those earnest, big blue eyes of yours. You really look like a modern-day version of Josephine Mabry."

Amanda crashed into the coffee table. She flailed her arms in a desperate attempt to regain her balance.

Only Michelle's quick reflexes kept her from falling. "Careful." She still held on to Amanda's arm but gentled her grip. "You all right?"

"Yes. Thanks." Amanda knew she was gaping, but she couldn't help it. Was Josephine Mabry really her favorite actress, or had Michelle just said that to flatter her? No. She couldn't know. And Amanda believed her when she said she wasn't one to use pretty lines just to flatter people. She sank onto the couch and swallowed two Tylenol. "You mentioning Josephine Mabry just caught me by surprise."

Michelle sat next to her and finally relinquished her hold on Amanda's arm. She leaned back and chuckled. "What, you thought I just watch movies like *Terminator* and *Rocky*, maybe with a bit of sports and porn thrown in?"

Heat shot into Amanda's face. Michelle wasn't the stereotypical butch—if such a thing even existed—so she really had to stop making stupid assumptions. Ignoring her blush, she held Michelle's gaze. "That's not what I meant. It's just that you're not exactly in the typical age group for a fan."

Michelle fluffed her short hair. "I'll have you know I've got two gray hairs already. And I've been a fan for twenty-five years."

"Uh-huh. Sure."

"God, you Hollywood people are a mistrustful bunch. Twenty-five years, I swear." Michelle held up three fingers in a Scout's honor gesture. "I watched all her movies with my grandfather when I was a kid. I think he had a crush on Ms. Mabry. Well, and maybe, just maybe I had a tiny crush on her too. Who could blame us? She was quite the looker in her day."

"Yes," Amanda said, "she was."

"Are you a fan too?" Michelle asked.

Amanda smiled. "Well, I guess you could say that. She's my grandmother."

Michelle's eyes widened. "Seriously?"

Amanda nodded.

The leather creaked as Michelle turned toward her on the couch. Her knee almost touched Amanda's thigh, but by now, her proximity wasn't as uncomfortable as before. "Wow, that's amazing. I feel a bit starstruck all of a sudden." The slightest bit of color dusted her cheeks.

Cute, Amanda thought and then shook her head. "I'm not the star. My grandmother is."

"Yeah, but you're an actress too, and I bet given the chance, you'd be just as good. What did she think about you becoming an actress?"

"I guess she's got conflicted feelings about it," Amanda said.

"Really? I'd have thought she would be as proud as a peacock of its tail feathers."

Amanda chuckled. "She is. If there were an Oscar for commercials, she would try to get me nominated."

The laugh lines around Michelle's eyes deepened. "So where do the conflicted feelings come in?"

"She knows the business," Amanda said, surprising herself with how willingly she answered this stranger's questions. "Most actresses never make it in Hollywood, and if they do, it's at a price. If you want to make a living as an actress, you'll have to take parts you don't want, work with people you don't like, and smile through it all. Some people even say you have to sell a piece of your soul to make it in Hollywood."

"I never got the impression that your grandmother did that." Michelle turned a bit more so that she was fully facing Amanda and laid her left arm along the back of the couch. "I mean, she made some movies that were highly controversial in their time, and she refused to let herself be typecast as a demure damsel or a seductress."

Amanda nodded. "And that's why few people other than you and your grandfather have ever heard of her. She won a National Society of Film Critics Award for Best Actress, but she never starred in blockbusters. She didn't care for fame or money; she just wanted to act. But then, she had a husband who made good money, and she knows I'll never have that. That's why she worries about me."

"So she knows you're gay?" A blush crept up Michelle's neck. "I mean…if you are gay. Just because you told that guy in the bar you're a lesbian and couldn't keep your hands off me when you were smashed, I shouldn't assume that…"

For once, Amanda wasn't the flustered one. She smiled. "Relax. I'm gay. And yes, my grandmother knows. She was the first person I came out to."

"And she's fine with it?"

"She says if that's what makes me happy, then she's all for it."

Michelle casually touched Amanda's shoulder. "That's what my grandfather said to me too. It's a shame those two never met. They would have made a great couple."

Amanda considered it for a moment. If Michelle's grandfather had married her grandmother, that would make them siblings or cousins. She shook her head. The longer she talked to Michelle, the more she liked her— but it wasn't in a sisterly way. The thought took her by surprise. *You're not attracted to her, are you?* No, of course she wasn't. Besides, she was too hungover to feel anything but nauseated. "I bet they would have liked each other," she said, "but I really can't imagine my grandmother with anyone but my grandfather."

"I know what you mean," Michelle said. "I can't imagine my grandfather with anyone but my grandmother either."

Silence spread between them, but this time, it wasn't uncomfortable.

After a while, Michelle pointed at the wall of DVDs. "Do you want to watch one of your grandmother's movies? I have them all."

Amanda glanced at her watch. She had more than enough time, but was it really a good idea to hang out here for much longer? After everything that Michelle had done for her, she didn't want to overstay her welcome.

"It's just an offer," Michelle said when Amanda kept hesitating. "I can drive you to your car now if you want, but it might not be a bad idea to let the residual alcohol wear off and give the Tylenol some time to kick in."

Finally, Amanda shrugged. "Sure, why not?" She hadn't seen her grandmother's movies in a while, and if she were at home now, she wouldn't do much beyond hanging out on the couch either.

"Which one?"

"How about *Spur of the Moment*?"

"Good choice. It's my favorite. Nothing beats a feisty woman taking on a bunch of unscrupulous land speculators." Michelle got up, picked a DVD out of the shelf without having to search for it, and headed over to the large flat-screen TV in the corner. On the way back from the DVD player, she hesitated in front of the recliner but then returned to the couch and sat next to Amanda again. "Want to do the honors?" Bowing as if she were handing over a scepter, she held out the remote control.

"Thank you, kind...um...lady." Their fingers brushed as Amanda reached for the remote control. She bit her lip and started the movie.

When the closing credits rolled across the TV screen, Amanda realized that her headache was now just a dull pressure instead of a constant throbbing. She had kicked off her shoes and curled her legs under her, surprising herself with how comfortable she felt in Michelle's living room. Their shoulders were touching—and probably had been during half of the movie.

Michelle moved a few inches to the right, away from Amanda, as if she only now realized it too. She turned her head and trailed her gaze over every inch of Amanda's face. "I wasn't imagining things. You look a lot like your grandmother."

Amanda blinked. "Yeah?" She liked to think so, but most people thought she was a carbon copy of her mother, who looked nothing like Grandma. "You really think so?"

"Of course. You have this..." Michelle reached out as if to touch Amanda's cheek with one fingertip. At the last moment, she withdrew her hand. "Um, the curve of your cheekbones is exactly like hers. And your smile."

They stared at each other.

Amanda's skin seemed to heat beneath Michelle's intense gaze.

Then Michelle looked away and cleared her throat. "How's your head?"

A little confused. But, of course, that wasn't what Michelle was asking. "I'm fine," Amanda said. She gulped down the remainder of her water.

"All right. Then let's go." Michelle turned off the TV, and they headed for the door.

Amanda smirked. At least one stereotype was true—Michelle's means of transportation was an SUV.

"So why doesn't the promising grandchild of the grande dame of romantic movies believe in love?" Michelle asked as she unlocked the car and held the passenger-side door open for Amanda.

Amanda waited until Michelle got in on her side and started the SUV before she answered, "Who said I don't believe in love?"

Michelle waited for another car to pass and pulled out of the driveway. While she expertly navigated the winding roads of the Hollywood Hills, she spared a quick glance over at Amanda. "You do?"

Was there a hopeful tone in her voice?

Amanda mentally shook her head. No, they had established once and for all that they weren't interested in each other. "Well, there was this week when my girlfriend left me for a double-D bimbo from a Brazilian telenovela, but other than that, sure, I believe in love."

"Then why did you attend the Anti-Valentine's Day party?"

Michelle's hands resting on the steering wheel looked sure and strong. For some reason, Amanda kept studying them, taking in the long fingers and the tendons playing in the back of her hands. Resolutely, she directed her gaze at the taillights of the car in front of them. "I don't believe in the commercialized version of love. Two friends of mine set me up with the only other lesbian they know, just because they thought I'd find eternal love on Valentine's Day. Needless to say it was a disaster."

"Ah." Michelle nodded as if she had been through dates like that too. "I'll never get why people think two lesbians will inevitably fall in love just because they're both gay."

"Me neither." Even Val, who had seemed like just her type, hadn't turned out to be a good match for her. "And you? What brought you to the Anti-Valentine's Day party?" Amanda asked, finally allowing herself to look over at Michelle again.

"All those sexy photos at work made me feel like I'm the only single woman on earth," Michelle said. "The party seemed like a good remedy."

Amanda quirked her eyebrows. Sexy photos at work? What the hell did she do for a living?

Michelle slowed when they reached Sunset Boulevard, where traffic seemed to crawl. She glanced at Amanda and then back at the street. "Don't look at me like that." She chuckled. "I'm not some pervert who reads *Playboy* at work when the boss isn't looking. I'm a photographer. A lot of customers came in this week to take erotic photos for their significant other."

"Ah. So all the photos in your house are yours? I mean, you took them?"

"Yes, they're mine. Well, except for the one I'm in. One of my employees took that one."

The images of the growling tiger and the age-spotted hands cradling a baby were still vivid in Amanda's memory. She whistled quietly. "Wow, you're good."

Michelle took one hand off the steering wheel and brushed her fingernails over her T-shirt. "Thank you. That's what all the women say after spending the night with me."

Snorting, Amanda nudged her with an elbow. "Show-off."

Michelle nudged her back and grinned. "Hey, don't knock it till you've tried it."

"Well, I did try it...or at least I started to." Amanda smirked and shrugged. "Seems it wasn't very memorable."

"Ouch." Michelle clutched her chest. "You could seriously harm a girl's ego, you know?"

"Somehow, I don't think there's much danger of that." Michelle seemed to have a healthy self-confidence, but it didn't tip over into arrogance, as it did with a lot of the actresses and show business people Amanda knew.

When they reached the now-deserted parking lot of the club, Michelle slowed the SUV. "Where are you parked?"

"Just across the street. You can let me out here."

Michelle pulled into the parking lot and turned off the engine.

Silence filled the car for a few moments.

Amanda fiddled with her seat belt before she managed to strip it off. She struggled to find the right words. "Thank you for rescuing me last night and for not kicking my hungover, bitchy self out this morning."

"You're very welcome." The expression in Michelle's brown eyes was sincere. "Just try to take better care of yourself next time."

"I will." Although the situation had ended up all right, Amanda didn't plan on a repeat of last night. *Okay, everything's said. Now get your hungover ass home.* She reached for the lever that opened the door.

"There's a way to make sure, you know?"

Amanda turned back around. "Excuse me?"

"Oh, you know how it is," Michelle said. "As soon as the next Valentine's Day comes around, your happily partnered friends will start playing Cupid again. They'll try to make sure you have a date for Valentine's Day."

Amanda scrunched up her face. "Maybe I'll book a cruise in February. I heard Antarctica is nice that time of year."

"That works too, but there are cheaper ways."

"Joining a convent?"

Michelle laughed. "Nothing quite so extreme. No, let's make a deal. If we're both still single next February, we'll go out with each other on Valentine's Day."

Amanda narrowed her eyes and regarded her. Was she joking, or did she really mean it?

A smile still played around Michelle's full lips, but her gaze was steady and serious.

"But I don't date butch women, and you don't date actresses."

Michelle shrugged. "Well, maybe we should both broaden our repertoires. Besides, I'm not proposing marriage. One date." She winked at Amanda. "I even promise to make sure you're not ordering drinks with names like mind eraser. So what do you say?"

Amanda considered it for a moment. Her date with Val, a feminine woman who seemed just her type, had been a catastrophe. No matter what, going out with Michelle just once couldn't be worse than that. "All right," she said. "And I promise not to grope you again."

"Damn," Michelle said.

Amanda elbowed her but couldn't help smiling.

"Um, I meant…deal."

They shook hands, holding on for a heartbeat longer than strictly necessary.

Finally, Amanda let go.

Before she could open the door, Michelle got out of the SUV and did it for her.

"Thanks," Amanda said.

Michelle reached into her pocket and pulled out her wallet. "Here's my card. Call me, and we can meet to talk about the details of our date."

"You want to go on a date to plan our date? Correct me if I'm wrong, but wouldn't that make it two dates?"

"Oh, no," Michelle said, not quite pulling off an innocent expression. "Let's just call it...rehearsal."

"Mmhmm." Amanda decided to let it go. If she was honest with herself, she had to admit that she would like to see Michelle before next year. It would give her a chance to thank her by paying for dinner. She took the card Michelle held out and studied it. Michelle V. Osinski. Photographer.

"So," Michelle jingled her keys, "see you soon, then."

"Yes. Until soon. And thanks again for everything."

One last nod and a smile, then Michelle rounded the SUV and got in on the driver's side. She reached out to close the door.

"Michelle," Amanda called.

Michelle paused and looked up. "Yes?"

"What does the V stand for?"

"Excuse me?"

Amanda lifted the card. "Your middle name."

"Ah." Michelle wrinkled her nose as if smelling something bad. "Veronica."

Not Valentine. Amanda smiled and decided to take it as a good omen.

"Why?" Michelle asked.

"Oh, nothing. Just curious. Drive carefully."

"Shouldn't be a problem now that no one's groping me." Grinning, Michelle closed the door, put on the seat belt, and turned the key in the ignition.

Amanda waved and watched until the SUV's taillights disappeared in the distance before she headed to her car. Another flyer advertising the Anti-Valentine's Day party was stuck behind her windshield wiper. She pulled it free and crumpled it up. Next year, she wouldn't need it.

CHAPTER 3

A HUNGRY CAT AND THE blinking red light of her answering machine greeted Amanda as she entered her apartment and kicked the door closed with her heel. She scratched Mischief behind one ear and listened to his scolding all the way to the kitchen. "Yeah, yeah, I know I'm a bad mom, and if you had hands instead of paws, you would have called the Society for the Prevention of Cruelty to Animals." She put a bowl of cat food on the floor and watched him gobble it up. "Come to think of it, if you had hands, you would have called a restaurant that delivers buffalo wings."

With one emergency taken care of, she leaned against the kitchen counter and flipped through the stack of junk mail. "Baroness de Rutherford, clairvoyant, will give you the wonderful gift of seeing your future." She snorted. One hundred dollars an hour wasn't what she'd call a gift. Besides, she didn't need a clairvoyant to know who had tried to reach her—very likely, Kathryn had called to tell her that someone else had gotten the lead in the horror movie she had auditioned for.

Sighing, she walked toward the answering machine.

When her cell phone started ringing to the tones of Madonna's "Hollywood," she nearly dropped the stack of junk mail. She lifted the phone to her ear without glancing at the display. "Hi, Kath. I was just about to call you."

"Where have you been? I called your apartment and your cell all morning, but all I got was your answering machine. Don't tell me you went home with your date from hell after all!"

"Good afternoon to you too, and thanks for asking how your favorite actress is."

"Yeah, yeah, yeah. So?" Kathryn stretched out the word as if it had five syllables.

Amanda strolled over to the living room and threw herself down onto the worn leather couch. "No, I didn't go home with Val."

There was a moment of silence.

If she were a bloodhound, she'd be sniffing now. For some reason, her agent always seemed to know when there was something Amanda wasn't telling her.

"But?" Kathryn asked. "Don't tell me she went home with you."

"God, no. If I had taken her home with me, we'd be looking for a priest willing to perform a lesbian wedding right about now."

"Not a good idea. You look awful in white."

"Thanks. Is there a reason you called other than to give me a hard time?"

"Well, I have good news."

Amanda sat up. A tingle of anticipation rushed through her. Had she gotten the role in that horror movie after all?

"I also have some bad news," Kathryn added. "Which do you want first?"

After the night and the morning she'd had, nothing could disturb her anymore. "Let's get it over with. Give me the bad news first."

"I got a call from Max Benton first thing this morning. He said it was a close call, but they gave the female lead role to someone else. I'm sorry, sweetie."

Amanda slumped against the back of the couch, rubbing her forehead as the headache from this morning made a reappearance. "Who got the part?"

Kathryn coughed but didn't answer for several seconds.

"Don't tell me. Lizzy, right?" Since they had split up two years ago, her ex made it a point to audition for the same roles as Amanda did. She sighed. Maybe Michelle was right. Dating actresses was a bad idea.

"I'm sorry," Kathryn said again.

"I'll get over it. So what's the good news?"

"They have an opening for a bit part."

"Let me guess. They want me to play the monster."

Kathryn chuckled. "Not quite. You'd be a dog walker."

Great. Amanda had read the script and knew the dog walker wouldn't survive the first five minutes of the movie. "I told you I wouldn't work with animals again after that commercial with the camel." She rubbed the scar that seemed to itch beneath her blouse. An image of showing off that scar to Michelle and half of the club flashed through her mind.

"Come on," Kathryn said. "It's a tiny Chihuahua. Didn't your grandmother once face down a lion in one of her movies? Now that's star quality!"

Amanda rolled her eyes. "I don't think being eaten by a giant lizard while chasing after Fifi will catapult me to instant stardom."

"Probably not, but you do have two lines of dialogue and will be listed in the credits. Maybe some other casting director will notice you."

"Okay, okay. Tell them I'll do it. Any other calls?"

"One from Rob," Kathryn said. "He wanted to know how your date went."

"Why didn't he call me?"

"He did, but you didn't pick up either of your phones."

Because I was passed out in a stranger's bedroom. Amanda rubbed her heated cheeks.

"He thinks you didn't answer because you were busy basking in the afterglow of great sex with Val," Kathryn said.

Amanda snorted. "Hardly. I was busy basking in the afterglow of half a dozen mind erasers."

"Mind erasers?"

"It's a mix of vodka, coffee liqueur, and—"

"I know what it is, but I've never known you to drink vodka."

"Not since spending most of my twenty-first birthday worshipping the porcelain goddess," Amanda said, grimacing at the memory. "But if you had been out on a date like that, believe me, you would have needed a drink too."

"One drink? You said half a dozen. Do I have to do any damage control to protect the image of my favorite client?"

Amanda's memory of last night was still a little fuzzy. Who knew what she would have done if Michelle hadn't taken her home with her? The more she thought about it, the more grateful she became. "No damage control necessary. The paparazzi aren't interested in taking embarrassing pictures of wannabe actresses playing lizard fodder in third-rate horror movies."

"Ooooh. Maybe the paparazzi aren't, but I am." Kathryn's voice vibrated with curiosity. "Come on. Tell me. What did you do?"

"Nothing much." Amanda studied her nails.

"That's exactly what the last client I fired said, after being caught urinating in the fountains of the Bellagio and getting into a fistfight with his co-star."

Amanda frowned. She hadn't heard about that. "What client was that?"

"Don't change the topic. Tell me what you did."

No way out. Kath was as curious as a cat and about as stubborn as one too. She wouldn't let it go. "I got drunk and went home with a woman." Hastily, Amanda added, "But nothing happened." Well, nothing but one pretty hot kiss and some groping on Amanda's part. By Hollywood standards, that *was* nothing.

"Sure," Kathryn said in a sarcastic tone. "That's what my third ex-husband said too when I caught him with that blonde bimbo."

"Hey, no cutting remarks about blondes, please. And I swear, nothing happened."

"Why not? Was she straight or something?"

Amanda chuckled. Not even her grandmother would have mistaken Michelle for straight. "Thanks for your confidence in my seductive powers. No, she's as gay as they come. She's just too honorable to sleep with a drunken woman." Yes, that was a good word to describe Michelle—honorable.

"Good for her," Kathryn said. "So will you meet her again?"

Amanda pulled Michelle's card from the pocket of her slacks and trailed her finger over the name. "I don't know." Part of her was fascinated by Michelle, but another part was sure that it'd never work out.

"Oh, come on. Finding an honorable woman in Hollywood is about as rare as finding a virgin in a harem. Why don't you give her a ch—?"

The ringing of Amanda's landline interrupted.

Saved by the bell. "Sorry, Kath, I have to go. It's probably my grandmother. I promised I'd come over after my shift at the juice bar."

"All right. Say hi to my favorite actress for me."

"I thought I was your favorite actress?"

"Uh…" Kathryn cleared her throat. "Shouldn't you pick up the phone?"

Laughing, Amanda said good-bye and pressed the end button on her cell phone.

"I'm so sorry, honey," her grandmother said instead of a greeting. "I just read on the *Hollywood Insider* blog that they gave your role to that horrible Sleazy."

Amanda suppressed a giggle. "Her name is Lizzy, Grandma; you know that." Her grandmother wasn't all that far off, though. Amanda had the sneaking suspicion that Lizzy had gotten comfortable on more than a few casting couches, even during their short-lived relationship.

"They don't know what they're missing. Now the scariest thing in that movie will be the acting."

Ice clinked on the other end of the line, and Amanda could imagine her grandmother setting down a glass of bourbon on the coffee table next to her iPad. "The doctor said you're not supposed to be drinking."

Her grandmother huffed. "What does that kid know? I'm eighty-two. It won't be the bourbon that kills me."

Amanda hated to even think about her grandmother dying, so she quickly changed the subject and said the first thing that came to mind, "I met a woman yesterday."

"I know," her grandmother said. "I was the one who encouraged you to go out on Valentine's Day instead of watching reruns of *The Golden Girls* with an old woman."

"I like watching *The Golden Girls* with you. Besides, I'm not talking about Val, the woman Rob and Kathryn set me up with."

"You aren't? So you met two women in one night? Ooh la la! You're clearly taking after me."

Amanda snorted. "Grandma, you never even looked at a man other than Grandpa."

"True," her grandmother said in a dreamy tone. Ice clinked as if she were swirling her glass. "So who was this woman you met?"

"Her name is Michelle."

"I once played a honky-tonk girl with that name," her grandmother said.

Amanda chuckled as she imagined Michelle in a frilly dance hall dress. The mental image seemed all wrong. She liked her much better in jeans and a tight muscle shirt. The thought surprised her, but then she shrugged and admitted to herself that Michelle was a good-looking woman.

"So?" her grandmother drawled when Amanda stayed silent. "Tell me more about her."

What could she say about Michelle? "I don't know her that well. I just know that she's a photographer. A really good one. She's got good manners, a big family, and a kitchen that could house my entire apartment."

"That's more than I knew about your grandfather when I married him."

"I'm not gonna marry her."

"I'm not talking about marriage," her grandmother said. "But she sounds nice. Will you see her again?"

Why did everybody keep asking her that? She didn't have an answer yet. "I don't know. She's nice, but..." Amanda shrugged. "She's not really my type."

"What do you mean? You said she has good manners and a career of her own. Isn't that what you want in a partner?"

"Yes, but..." Amanda tugged on her hair with her free hand. "I like feminine women, and Michelle is... Well, she's not. She looks pretty butch, actually."

Her grandmother seemed to consider this for a moment. "And that's why you won't go out with her again? Mandy, for a gay girl, you sound pretty prejudiced."

Amanda gaped at the photo of her grandmother on her bookshelf. "I'm not prejudiced." Or was she? Admittedly, some of her ideas about butch women had turned out to be pretty stereotypical and didn't fit Michelle at all. But still the fact remained that she'd never been attracted to a butch before. "I just know my type, and it's not butch women."

"Your grandfather wasn't my type either."

"What? I always thought it was love at first sight."

"It was—for him. But it took a day or two for me. When I was young, I mooned over James Dean and Marlon Brando. I liked those tough, brooding rebel types, and God knows, your grandfather wasn't like that."

Amanda's gaze wandered to the next framed photo on her shelf, which showed her grandparents on their silver wedding anniversary. They were holding hands, looking into each other's eyes, ignoring the photographer. She studied her grandfather's work-worn hands and the deep laugh lines around his eyes. What she remembered most about him was his gentleness and his unconditional honesty—

so different from the partying, phony Hollywood actors swarming her grandmother when she had been young.

"You hit the jackpot when you met Grandpa," Amanda said. "But that doesn't mean that I'll be as lucky. Lately, all of my dates seem like the auditions I go to—I hope for the big relationship break, but all I get are short-lived bit roles."

"That's because you're typecasting," her grandmother said.

Amanda frowned, even though she'd been the one to start using acting metaphors for her love life. "Typecasting?"

"You keep dating gals like that Sleazy—"

"Lizzy."

The ice in her grandmother's drink clinked again, as if she had just taken a big sip of bourbon. "Yeah, her and those other ladies you dated."

"Christ, you make it sound as if there'd been a string of them."

"No. That's not what I'm saying. But they're all the same type: all of them dazzling beauties and most of them fellow actresses. And you know how actresses are. They're after fame and fun, not after love and loyalty—present company excluded, of course."

"Of course." Amanda had to admit that her grandmother was right. "So you think I should stop typecasting my dates?"

"It's worth a try, isn't it?"

Amanda fiddled with the card in her pocket. "Maybe I'll call her," she finally said. "She's a fan of yours after all, so at least she's got taste."

"Ooh, she's a fan? Then bring her over. I'd love to meet her."

"So you can get out that photo album and show her embarrassing nude pictures of me? No, thanks."

"Nude pictures? You were an adorable three-year-old reenacting *Flipper* in an inflatable pool!"

"All right, but still. If I really go out with her, I don't want to scare off the poor woman by introducing her to my family on the second date."

Her grandmother hummed her agreement. "I suppose that would be too fast, even for two lesbians."

After finding out Amanda was gay, her grandmother had watched every lesbian movie and TV show ever made—even though she loudly complained about the acting in most of them—and she constantly baffled Amanda's friends with her knowledge of pop culture references to toaster ovens and U-Hauls.

"I have to get going," Amanda said. "My shift starts in an hour. I'll come over after work and bring you some juice."

"Drive carefully. And call that woman."

"I will," Amanda said, not knowing which of her grandmother's requests she was referring to. She stared at her grandparents' photo for a moment longer and then kicked herself into motion and hurried to the bedroom to change.

Amanda lay with her knees pulled up to accommodate the cat curled up at the bottom of her bed. The phone in one hand, she rubbed her thumb across the battered card in her other hand. Was Michelle even still expecting her call? It had been a week since Valentine's Day after all.

"What do you think, Mischief? Should I call her or not?"

At the sound of her voice, Mischief lifted his head and blinked sleepily. "Meow."

"Is that a yes?"

"Mrrrauw."

"Guess it is, huh?" She played with one of the card's bent corners. Not that she really needed the card anymore. After calling Michelle three times in the past week—and always hanging up before she could pick up—she knew the number by heart. She hesitated with her thumb hovering over the first button. "Come on. Do it."

The worst that could happen was that she'd discover that Michelle wasn't her type at all and the attraction she had felt last week had been just a fluke, caused by too many mind erasers.

Determined, she typed in the number and, with her heart in her throat, lifted the phone to her ear.

After just one ring, her insecurities crept up again, and she moved her thumb to end the call, but the phone was picked up before she could do it.

"Hello?"

Amanda froze with her thumb over the end button. Why hadn't she rehearsed what she wanted to say? *Some actress you are.* "Uh, hi. This is Amanda."

"Hi, Amanda." Michelle's voice was warm and welcoming. "I wasn't sure you'd call."

Her frank honesty startled Amanda again, but she decided she liked it. "I wasn't sure either."

"I'm glad you did," Michelle said.

Silence filled the line while Amanda debated whether she should say the same.

"So, how's the acting biz treating you?" Michelle asked before Amanda's inner debate came to a conclusion. "Any big, mean camels in your professional life right now?"

Amanda laughed and relaxed back against her pillow. "No. There's a Chihuahua in my immediate future, but thank God, no camels."

"A Chihuahua? Is this for a dog food commercial?"

"No, it's a movie."

"Wow, that's great. Congratulations."

Amanda scratched her neck, embarrassed at the enthusiasm in Michelle's voice. "Nothing to get too excited about. It's just a bit role, and I die a horrible death five minutes in."

"Still, it's a start, right?"

"Guess it is." Amanda liked Michelle's positive attitude toward life. She cleared her throat and wondered how to ask out a butch woman. Wasn't the butch supposed to do the asking? Finally, she decided to toss all her preconceived notions overboard and just ask. "Listen, I'd really like to invite you to dinner as a small thank-you for all you did for me."

"You don't owe me anything." Chuckling, Michelle added, "But, of course, that doesn't mean I'm saying no to having dinner with you. Just tell me when and where, and I'll be there."

Strange how eager she was to get a date with Amanda. Hadn't she said she would never date another actress? Amanda wanted to ask what had happened to that resolution but chickened out. Instead, she heard herself say, "How about Friday? Would seven work?"

"Seven sounds perfect."

Amanda mentally flipped through the list of restaurants Michelle might like. There wasn't exactly a shortage of restaurants in LA. "How about the Mexican restaurant on Oxnard Street? Do you like it spicy?"

"Oh, yeah. The spicier, the better." Michelle laughed.

The low, sensual sound sent a shiver down Amanda's back, as if Michelle had trailed a finger along her spine. "Food," she said, glad that they were on the phone, so Michelle couldn't see her blush. "I'm talking about food."

"Of course. What did you think I was talking about?" Michelle was still chuckling. "But seriously, Mexican food is fine. Do you want me to pick you up?"

"Since I invited you, good manners dictate that I be the one to pick you up, don't you think?"

Michelle hesitated for a second, as if not used to being the one picked up. "I'd like that," she finally said. "Do you still remember where I live?"

"I think so."

"Are you sure? You didn't exactly pay much attention the last time we drove to my house—at least not to your surroundings."

Heat crawled up Amanda's neck. She still couldn't believe she had groped Michelle in the car—even though she had to admit to being curious about how those muscular thighs would feel under her soft-looking, worn jeans. She cleared her throat. "I'll find it." She still had Michelle's card with her address, so she would look it up online, just to be sure.

"Good," Michelle said, a smile in her voice. "I look forward to Friday, then."

"Me too." It wasn't one of the little white lies used so often in Hollywood. For the first time in longer than she cared to admit, Amanda found herself looking forward to a date. Long after they had said good-bye, she lay on her bed, smiling, the phone pressed to her ear.

CHAPTER 4

MICHELLE WAS SITTING ON THE top step of her white front porch when Amanda pulled up in front of her house half an hour late. *Oh, shit. Not the way to make a good first impression.* But then she remembered that Michelle's first impression of her had been that of a drunken stranger grabbing and kissing her.

As soon as she stopped her fifteen-year-old Mazda, Michelle jumped up and rushed down the stairs toward her. "I was beginning to worry," she said as she got in on the passenger side. "I thought you got lost after all."

That hadn't been the problem. Thanks to Google, Amanda had found the place without any difficulties, but it had taken her forever to get ready for their date. She had obsessed over her hair and tried on five different outfits—only to end up wearing the first one she'd tried on. "No, sorry, I just...uh...lost track of time."

Michelle studied her with one raised eyebrow. A slow grin spread across her face.

Amanda crossed her arms and gave her a faux strict look. "What's that grin for? Don't you believe me?"

"Grin? What grin?" Michelle tried to wipe the grin off her face and look innocent—without much success.

"You're not trying to out-act an actress, are you?"

"Me?" Michelle touched her chest. "No, never."

"Good, because you're not fooling me, Michelle Veronica Osinski."

Michelle winced at the use of her middle name. Then the grin left her face, and she regarded Amanda seriously. "I'm not trying to fool you. With me, what you see is what you get."

Their gazes met and held for a few seconds.

"Before I forget to mention it," Michelle finally said. "You look beautiful."

Tugging at the hemline of her dress, Amanda shrugged. "Thanks. My grandmother always says you can't go wrong with a little black dress if you're a blonde."

"Wise woman. Shall we?"

As Michelle reached for the seat belt, Amanda used the moment when she was distracted to study her. In a pair of black dress pants and a black vest, she looked sleek and elegant. Her ivory-colored shirt contrasted with her tanned skin and made her eyes look even darker. When she had the seat belt on, she tugged on her cuffs and touched her short hair as if to make sure it wasn't sticking up at crazy angles.

Amanda grinned. Good to know that she wasn't the only one who was a bit nervous.

"What's that grin for?" Michelle asked as she turned toward her.

"Grin? What grin?" Amanda drew heavily on her acting skills to make herself sound innocent, doing a much better job than Michelle had.

Michelle reached over and nudged her arm. "Uh-huh. You're not fooling me, Amanda I-don't-know-your-middle-name Clark."

At the touch, a tingle ran through Amanda's arm. "Good." For once, she wanted to have dinner with someone without having to pretend. After one last glance at the woman next to her, she started the car and pulled out of the driveway. "It's Josephine, by the way."

"Uh, what?"

"My middle name. It's Josephine."

"Oh, cool. After your grandmother, I assume?"

Amanda nodded. In later years, her parents had cursed themselves for that decision, since her grandmother was such a bad influence in their opinion. Sighing, she decided to focus on the present and leave the past in the past.

"Have you decided on something to drink?" the waiter asked.

Amanda considered it for a moment. On her date with Valentine, she had chugged down red wine as if there were no tomorrow, hoping it would help her survive the evening. Tonight, that wasn't necessary. Michelle was pleasant company. During the drive to the restaurant, she had regaled her with funny anecdotes about her customers until Amanda's sides and face ached from laughing so hard.

"They have a great peach and mango margarita," Michelle said when Amanda hesitated.

Amanda shook her head. "Just some sparkling water with lime, please," she said to the waiter before turning back to Michelle. "I'm driving after all, and I have a feeling that drinking around you is dangerous."

"Me? Hey, the last time you were drinking, I was the one being grabbed and kissed senseless—not that I'm complaining, mind you."

The waiter cleared his throat next to them. "And what can I get you, sir?"

Amanda blinked and stared at him. Was he blind? Yes, Michelle had short hair and preferred more masculine clothes, but with her sensuous mouth and her long lashes, she couldn't be mistaken for a man.

Before Amanda could tell him to open his eyes and get a clue, Michelle said calmly, "It's ma'am. And I'll have what the lady is having."

Mumbling an apology, the waiter hurried off.

Amanda reached across the table to touch Michelle's hand for a moment. "I'm sorry."

Michelle just grinned. "Don't worry. I'm used to it. People see what they want to see."

"Doesn't it bother you?" Few things seemed to bother Michelle, and Amanda decided that she liked her calm energy, so different from many of the high-maintenance Hollywood divas she knew.

"It used to, especially when women started to scream whenever I entered the showers at my gym. Now I just strip down as soon as I enter the locker room." Michelle chuckled. "That way, if anyone starts screaming, it's just because they're crazy about my abs."

A mental image of Michelle's abs—and the rest of her naked body—flashed through Amanda's mind, making her flush. She hid her face behind the menu and tried to focus on the listed dishes before peeking back up at Michelle. "What looks good to you?"

Michelle glanced across the table and let her gaze slide over Amanda in a slow perusal. "You do. You're pretty cute when you're blushing. Or are you talking about food again?" she asked, smiling.

Rolling her eyes, Amanda slapped her hand with the menu. "Of course I am. Don't pretend you didn't know." Despite her complaints, she had to admit that Michelle's open admiration was flattering.

"Okay, okay, I—"

The waiter interrupted as he stepped up to their table with their sparkling water. "May I take your order?"

That guy was seriously beginning to annoy Amanda. On her date with Val, she'd have wished for a waiter to interrupt them, but not now. "I'd like to have the carne asada with patatas fritas, please," Amanda said.

The waiter turned to Michelle.

"For me, the enchiladas de pollo, please."

As soon as the waiter had left, Amanda leaned forward. "You're not ordering one of the cheapest dishes on the menu because you're thinking of a starving actress's budget, are you?"

"I'm ordering the enchiladas because I had them before and they were fantastic."

With the slight wink on Michelle's face, Amanda couldn't tell whether it was the complete truth, so she decided to just take her at face value. "You've been here before?"

Michelle nodded. "It's been a while, though. They used to offer cooking classes, but then the owner changed and they don't do that anymore."

"You really like to cook, don't you?"

"I love it," Michelle said, her lashes lowered as if focusing inward. "The scent, the taste, the textures... It's such an intimate, sensual experience. And if I cook for someone I love, it's even more special." She looked up, and her intense gaze met Amanda's.

Amanda trailed one index finger over her fork. "Hmm. I never thought of cooking that way." She usually just threw a salad together, warmed up some soup, and was done with it.

"Then you're not doing it right," Michelle said, grinning. "I'll have to cook for you some time."

"You mean some time when I'm not hungover and just picking at your toast."

Michelle laughed. "That'd be a plus, yes. So, what do you like to do in your spare time?"

Amanda toyed with her napkin. Usually, she didn't admit to her dates that she spent most of her free time losing at bridge to a bunch of eighty-year-olds. It made her sound like such a stick-in-the-mud. "Well, between my acting gigs and working at a juice bar, there's not much time for—"

Michelle's hand covering hers stopped her. Michelle just looked at her, encouraging, not accusing.

After blowing out a breath, Amanda said, "To tell you the truth, I spend most of my free time with my grandmother. Not doing anything special, just helping her around the house, playing cards, keeping her company, you know?"

"Nothing wrong with that. I loved to hang out with my grandfather too and just watch him repair something," Michelle said, her voice so low and intimate that Amanda had to lean forward to hear her. "He used to be a mechanic. He could fix anything. People constantly brought him toasters, watches, radios, and other stuff that wasn't working anymore. I would just sit there and watch his hands. It was like magic."

Amanda looked down at the hand that was still covering hers. With its long fingers, Michelle's hand looked strong and capable too. She turned her hand and softly squeezed Michelle's fingers. Her skin tingled. *Magic.*

Again, the waiter interrupted when he stepped up to the table with their food.

Okay, it's official now. No tip for this guy. Amanda pulled her hand back so he could place the plates on the table.

When they began to eat, she found her attention drawn to Michelle's hands time and again. "That large photo next to your TV, the age-spotted hands cradling a baby...?"

Smiling, Michelle nodded. "That's my grandfather holding my oldest niece." Her face sobered. "He died before my other nieces and nephews were born."

A big lump formed in Amanda's throat, making it impossible to say anything or swallow the piece of grilled beef in her mouth.

"Hey, I didn't mean to ruin the mood," Michelle said after a few seconds of silence. "My grandfather had a good, long life, and he certainly wouldn't want us to sit around moping on our first date."

"First date?" Amanda shook her head. "This isn't a date, remember? You called it a rehearsal."

"Oh, yeah, right." Michelle scratched her head and looked across the table with a twinkle in her eyes. "Does that mean I won't get to kiss you goodnight later?"

The thought of kissing Michelle sent a flash of heat through Amanda. She reached for her water and took two big gulps, as if that would help her cool off. "Sorry to tell you, but there's no kissing at rehearsals."

"Unless you're shooting porn," Michelle said, grinning.

Amanda nearly choked on another sip of water. "I'm not doing that."

"Good for you," Michelle said, this time in a more serious tone. "So tell me more about yourself. Did you grow up in California?"

How different this evening was turning out to be. Usually, her dates didn't ask so many questions about her. Most blabbed on and on about themselves. *Well, this isn't a date, remember?* She picked up a piece of fried potato and chewed it before answering, "Do you really want to hear the sad story of my life?"

"I wouldn't have asked otherwise. But if you'd rather not tell me…"

"No, it's okay. It's just…" She pierced a square of meat with her fork but instead of eating, she just studied it.

"Not pleasant memories?" Michelle asked.

"Some of them are—up until I came out to my parents at sixteen and told them I wanted to become an actress. Hard to say what they hate more, me being an actress or me being a lesbian."

Without hesitation, Michelle reached across the table and squeezed her hand. "But your grandmother was fine with both?"

"Oh, yeah. She was my champion. She took me in when living with my parents became unbearable."

"And you've been an actress ever since?"

"Not quite," Amanda said. "I got a degree in social work first. My parents insisted on it, just in case my 'harebrained idea' of becoming an actress didn't work out. After finishing my degree and saving up some money, I decided to give myself five years. If I didn't have a big break by then, I'd go back to social work."

"How long has it been?"

"Four years, three months, and about ten days—not that I'm counting or anything." Amanda deftly cut off another piece of steak and chewed it.

With her fork hovering over her enchilada, Michelle looked at her. "Don't give up your dreams. When I first started out, a lot of people told me the last thing LA needs is another photographer, but fortunately, I was too stubborn to listen. The first few years, I had to take a lot of photos of screaming toddlers, spoiled celebrities, and overweight housewives trying to look sexy in teddies two sizes too small. I still do a few of those, but for the most part, I can now pretty much do whatever I want to."

"Which is?"

"Art photography. Photos like the ones you saw in my house."

Even though she had been hungover at the time, Amanda vividly remembered the large black-and-white prints in Michelle's house, a close-up of a growling tiger, a daisy growing out of a crack in the sidewalk, and the weathered face of an old man squinting into the sun. "I don't know much about photography, but even I can tell that they're great."

"Thanks," Michelle said with obvious delight.

"Are you showing your work in galleries?"

Michelle nodded. "I'm not Annie Leibovitz, but I sell quite well in some of the smaller galleries. You'll get to that point in your career too. Just promise me one thing."

Amanda set down her fork. "What?"

"That you'll still go out on a date with me when you're a famous film star."

"This is not a date," Amanda reminded her, but she couldn't help smiling at Michelle's insistence.

Michelle shrugged. "Yeah, well, even big-time actresses have to have rehearsal partners, right?"

"Right," Amanda said and dug into her patatas fritas.

There were definite advantages to going out with someone who wasn't an actress or involved in the entertainment industry, Amanda decided as she shared a cheesecake flan and a piece of boca negra with Michelle.

Most of her previous dates carefully counted every calorie and didn't order dessert, or they complained with every bite about how much time they'd have to spend in the gym to make up for it.

Michelle, however, didn't seem to have any regrets. A sensual moan drifted across the table. Michelle's eyes closed as her lips wrapped around a forkful of chocolate cake. Her tongue flicked over her full bottom lip to remove a crumb from the corner of her mouth.

Amanda shifted in her chair. When Michelle opened her eyes, Amanda quickly wrenched her gaze away and busied herself dipping a spoonful of flan into the pecan cream sauce. The flavors of vanilla, lemon, and nuts exploded on her taste buds, and now it was her turn to moan.

When she looked up, about to offer Michelle a bite, Michelle's eyes, normally the color of the chocolate cake, had gone black, and she stared at Amanda's lips.

Slowly, her gaze still on Michelle, Amanda swallowed her bite of flan.

Desserts forgotten, they stared at each other.

The ringing of a cell phone interrupted the silence.

Dazed, Amanda needed a moment to figure out that it was hers. "Oh, I'm sorry. I forgot to turn it off."

"Go ahead and take the call. Could be Hollywood calling, right?" Michelle smiled, but it didn't look as if she was mocking her.

Amanda glanced at the display. Unknown caller. "I don't think so, but you never know. Are you sure?"

Michelle nodded.

Amanda accepted the call and lifted the cell phone to her ear. "Yes?"

"Hi, sweetheart. I know you're busy, and that's why you didn't call. So I thought I'd call and see when I should pick you up for our next date."

Just her luck. Instead of the call of her dreams, she had to get the call of her nightmares while she was having dinner with Michelle. She sighed and rubbed her eyes. "Listen, Val." She opened her mouth, about to make an excuse about how busy she was and that she had no time to date if she wanted to make it in Hollywood, but then decided to be honest. In the end, it would be less painful to make things clear once and for all. "You're a nice person and a good-looking woman, but there just wasn't any chemistry between us."

"How can you say that? There was plenty of—"

"Not for me. I'm sorry, Val, but there just wasn't."

"But maybe there will be if you give this…give us a chance. We're meant to be; can't you see that?"

"No," Amanda said gently, but firmly. "I'm sorry, but it wouldn't work."

After a moment of sniffling, Val said, "Is there someone else?"

Amanda glanced over at Michelle, who was keeping her gaze focused on her plate in a futile attempt not to listen in. "Well, I'm having dinner with someone right now, but—"

"You're cheating on me?" Valentine screeched.

Amanda covered her eyes with her free hand. "Please, calm down. I'm not cheating on you."

"But you just said—"

"I'm not cheating on you, because we were never in a relationship. We had one date. One date that I cut short because—" She stopped herself. *No. Don't be mean.* "Because I had to go comfort my agent when her husband broke up with her. I'm sorry, Val, but I'm not the soul mate you're looking for. I'm sure you'll find her eventually. Best of luck." She ended the call before Val could try to talk her out of it.

Michelle looked over at her. "Not that it's any of my business, but…what was that?"

"That was the reason I got smashed on Valentine's Day. Please don't think that I make a habit of—"

Amanda's phone started ringing again.

"Jesus. I'm so sorry, Michelle."

Michelle gave her a commiserating smile. "Some lesbians just don't get it, do they?"

"Let me just shut this thing off." As she fumbled with the phone, Amanda's gaze fell on the display. Her heart started beating faster, this time with worry. "I need to take this. It's my grandmother. She wouldn't call if it weren't important."

"Of course. Go ahead."

Amanda quickly pressed the button. "Are you okay, Grandma?"

"Oh, yes, of course. I'm fine, but this darned TV isn't."

Amanda blew out a breath. "You really scared me. I thought it was an emergency."

"Well, it is," her grandmother said. "There's no sound on my TV, and I'm not a lip-reader. Are you still on your date?"

Glancing over at Michelle, who had stopped eating, she said, "It's not a date, but yes, we're still at the restaurant."

"Oh, well. I wanted to watch the *Ellen* episode I taped this afternoon before I went to bed, but I guess it can wait till tomorrow. I'm sorry for interrupting. Enjoy the rest of the evening."

"Wait," Amanda said before her grandmother could hang up. "I'll come over and see if I can fix the TV after my...uh..."

"Your date that is not a date." Her grandmother chuckled.

Amanda rolled her eyes. "I'll be there in less than an hour, okay?"

"All right. Please drive carefully."

"I will." After ending the call, Amanda sent Michelle an apologetic glance. "I'm sorry. My grandmother usually doesn't call me while I'm on a...while I'm having dinner with someone, but it was an emergency. Kind of."

"Is she okay?" Michelle asked. Her forehead wrinkled in concern.

"She's fine, just a bit upset that she can't get her daily *Ellen* fix because the TV isn't working."

The wrinkles in Michelle's forehead smoothed, and new lines formed around her eyes as she laughed. "Your grandmother watches *The Ellen DeGeneres Show*? How cool is that?"

"A few years back, when Ellen hosted the Oscars for the first time, Grandma even cut her hair short, the way Ellen wears it, as a sign of her support."

They both laughed about that.

"I'm sorry to do this, but would you mind taking a cab home?" Amanda asked. "I need to go over to my grandmother's."

"You're not trying to get rid of me, are you?" Michelle smiled, but her tone was serious and shadows of hurt lurked in her eyes. "I mean, it's the oldest trick in the book, right? You have someone call, just in case the date is not going well, and pretend there's an emergency. Sounds like that's exactly how you got rid of that woman you went out with on Valentine's Day."

Amanda opened her mouth to assure her it wasn't like that, but Michelle shook her head.

"You don't need to do that with me," Michelle said. "If you want to leave, just—"

"No!" Amanda said so loudly that the people at the table next to theirs were starting to look over. Blushing, she ducked her head. "No, I swear that's not what's going on. I admit I used that trick to get rid of my date the evening we met, but this is different." She hadn't felt as if she needed rescuing at any time tonight. "There really is a problem with my grandmother's TV. I know that doesn't sound like a big deal, but for her, it is. Since my grandfather died four years ago, she always has the TV on. She says it helps her not to miss his voice so much. So I'd really like to see if I can fix it tonight."

Michelle studied her for a moment, her dark eyes probing into Amanda's.

Amanda didn't avert her gaze.

Finally, Michelle nodded. "All right. How about I come with you? Maybe I can help."

"I can't ask that of you."

"You're not asking—I'm offering. Now stop being so stubborn and say yes." Michelle reached across the table and nudged her. "Come on." She lowered her voice to a seductive purr. "You know you want it."

Amanda's cheeks heated, but she chose to ignore it. "Do you know how to fix a TV?"

"I watched my grandfather do it about a hundred times." Michelle wolfed down the rest of her chocolate cake and raised her hand to summon the waiter. "Come on. Let's go rescue a damsel in distress."

Amanda knew something fishy was going on as soon as her grandmother opened the door, dressed in the skirt and blouse she wore on bridge nights, even though it wasn't Tuesday. Grandma usually changed into her nightgown and robe after dinner if she wasn't expecting company. Had she dressed up, just in case she'd bring Michelle along?

"Hi, Grandma." She bent to kiss her grandmother's soft cheek and then stepped aside to let Michelle enter. "Grandma, this is Michelle Osinski. Michelle, this is my grandmother, Josephine—"

"Mabry. I know. It's an honor to meet you. I'm a big fan." Michelle stepped past Amanda and gently held Grandma's hand between both of hers. For a moment, she looked as if she was about to kiss it.

"I heard quite a lot about you too," Grandma said.

Michelle lifted one brow. "Oh, really? Is that so?" She sent Amanda a curious glance.

Amanda blushed. "Grandma, hush. Don't listen to her, Michelle. I didn't tell her a thing."

Her grandmother took Michelle's arm and tugged her toward the living room. "True, and that speaks volumes. So, tell me, dear, how did the two of you meet?"

Oh, shit. Amanda hurried after them. She didn't want her grandmother to know that Michelle had rescued her as she had stumbled about in a club's parking lot, too drunk to remember her own address. "Um, I... We..."

"We met at an Anti-Valentine's Day party," Michelle said before Amanda could stutter out a complete sentence.

"An Anti-Valentine's Day party?" her grandmother repeated. "I didn't even know there was such a thing."

"Yeah, well, what can I say?" Michelle shrugged. "I haven't been very lucky in love so far. But I hope that's about to change."

Grandma squeezed her arm with both hands. "I'm sure it will, dear."

"So let's take a look at the TV," Amanda said before they started making wedding plans.

Michelle led Grandma over to her armchair and, once she was safely seated, took off her vest and rolled up the sleeves of her ivory-colored shirt, instantly drawing Amanda's attention to her muscular forearms.

When her grandmother looked at her and grinned, Amanda wrenched her gaze away and checked out the TV instead. Pictures of today's news flickered across the screen, but there was no sound.

Without paying attention to the damage it might do to her elegant clothes, Michelle squeezed behind the TV stand in the corner of the room.

Amanda moved closer and craned her neck to be able to watch her.

Michelle slid her long fingers along the cables, checking for any damage or loose connectors.

Magic. Unbidden, images of those fingers sliding over her skin flashed through Amanda's mind.

"Hmm, weird," Michelle mumbled. "Everything seems to be just the way it's supposed to be, but I still can't get it to work. So much for inheriting my grandfather's skills. I bet he would have fixed it in two seconds flat."

"Let me see."

As Michelle slipped out from behind the TV, their bodies brushed.

Amanda's breath caught. She wanted to lean even closer, breathe in the scent of Michelle's cologne, and feel her heat, but under her grandmother's observant eyes, she hastily stepped past Michelle. Hidden behind the TV, she took a trembling breath. *Wow.* When had she last met a woman who made her weak in the knees like that, without even really touching her?

Hey, you're here to fix the TV, not to lust for a woman! With fingers that felt unsteady, she unplugged the A/V cable and connected it again.

Still no sound.

"I give up. I'm sorry, Grandma. I'll call someone to come over and look at the TV first thing tomorrow morning." When she climbed out from behind the TV stand, Michelle offered her a hand, and she grasped it gratefully, holding on to keep her balance.

Even once she was safely in the middle of the living room again, Michelle didn't let go. Not that Amanda minded. That strong, warm hand felt good against her own.

"That's all right. Don't worry about it, honey. I'll make do without *Ellen* for one night." Her grandmother reached out and patted Amanda's free hand.

As Amanda bent to kiss her grandmother goodnight, her gaze fell on the remote control on the coffee table.

Normally, it was buried beneath a stack of TV guides, celebrity gossip magazines, and puzzle books, but now it lay on top of the pile. It couldn't be that easy, could it? Probably not, but it was worth a try. She took the remote control, pointed it toward the TV, and pressed the mute button.

A news reporter's excited voice blared out of the TV's speakers.

"Oh my!" Her grandmother clapped her hands. "I must have accidentally pressed that button without realizing it."

Amanda narrowed her eyes at her, but her grandmother looked completely innocent. Then again, she hadn't been one of the most critically acclaimed actresses of the fifties and sixties for nothing.

She kissed her grandmother's cheek. "I'm on to you, you wily old woman," she whispered into her ear.

Her grandmother batted her big blue eyes at her. "Whatever do you mean, dear?"

Laughing, Amanda kissed her again and said goodnight before following Michelle to the door.

"I'm glad we could solve your grandmother's problem," Michelle said when Amanda started the car. "Even though I was no help at all."

"Oh, you helped her all right."

At the sarcastic tone of her voice, Michelle looked over at her. "What do you mean?"

"My grandmother is not one of those old ladies who are completely clueless about everything that has to do with technology. She's got a laptop, an iPad, and a computer with enough RAM to steer a spaceship."

Michelle frowned. "You mean…that harmless-looking old lady just pulled one over on us?"

"You bet she did. She wanted to check you out, so she found a way to lure us over to her house."

Michelle's laughter echoed through the car, a deep, low sound that made Amanda tingle all over. "She's something else, isn't she?"

Amanda smiled fondly. "That she is."

"And so is her granddaughter," Michelle said, her tone soft and earnest.

Amanda's gaze veered away from the street for a moment and met hers. Not sure how to respond to Michelle's words and the expression in her eyes, she quickly refocused her attention to the street.

When they reached Michelle's bungalow in the Hollywood Hills, Amanda stopped the car and turned off the engine.

For a few moments, they sat in silence.

"So," Amanda said when she couldn't stand to listen to her own too-loud breathing any longer.

Michelle looked at her, her gaze as soft as a touch. "So…"

The sudden sound of Madonna's "Hollywood" nearly made Amanda go through the roof of her car. "Christ." She clutched her chest. When she turned to grope in the backseat for her purse, her shoulder brushed Michelle's, starting that by now familiar tingling in every cell of her body again. Finally, she found the ringing cell phone and turned back around, instantly missing the warm touch. "Can we make this short, Kath?"

"Uh, yeah, sure. I just thought you'd want to hear the good news right away."

"What good news?" Amanda asked, more focused on the way the streetlamps threw shadows across the handsome planes of Michelle's face than on the phone call. "Did they hire me for that footed pajamas commercial?"

Kathryn laughed, sounding giddier than Amanda had ever heard her. "No. Better. Much, much, much better. You've heard of *Central Precinct*?"

"That hot new crime show that won three Emmys for its first season?"

"Yep, that's the one. Apparently, the female lead just quit—and they want you to replace her!"

For several seconds, Amanda just sat there and blinked. "But...but I didn't even audition for a role on that show."

"Doesn't matter. They want you, sight unseen."

"Oh, wow. That's...that's..." She dropped the phone onto her lap, bounced up and down in the driver's seat, and started screaming like a banshee.

"Uh, what's going on?" Michelle asked, her mouth quirking into a smile as she watched Amanda.

"They offered me a role as one of the leads on *Central Precinct*!" After one last bounce, Amanda whirled around and beamed at Michelle.

"What? Wow, that's great! Congratulations!"

Amanda laughed giddily. Feeling so happy that she wanted to embrace the whole wide world, she threw her arms around Michelle instead and kissed her.

For a second, Michelle stiffened.

Instantly, Amanda pulled back. "Oh God, I'm sorry. I didn't mean to... Christ, first I kiss you when I'm drunk and now—"

Michelle shut her up by pressing their lips together.

Heat flared through Amanda, and she wrapped her arms around Michelle to pull her closer. Drunk on happiness and the feeling of Michelle's lips against hers, she deepened the kiss and moaned as Michelle's warm tongue met hers. Her fingers slid up and into Michelle's short hair.

Finally, after a minute or two, she became aware of a tinny voice coming from the cell phone on her lap. Breathing heavily, she pulled her lips away from Michelle's and lifted the cell phone to her ear. "I've got to go, Kath. I'll call you tomorrow to get all the details," she said and hung up without waiting for a reply.

Then her lips were on Michelle's again.

Half an hour later, even the heat of Michelle's kisses couldn't make Amanda ignore the uncomfortable pressure of the middle console against her side any longer. She pulled back and leaned against the driver's seat, her gaze still on Michelle, drinking her in.

Michelle's chest was heaving and her hair was disheveled, making Amanda want to run her fingers through it. Slowly, Michelle lifted her hand and touched her own lips.

The gesture made Amanda want to kiss her again, but instead she reached over and brushed a bit of spiderweb off Michelle's shirt, which must have gotten stuck there when she had climbed behind the TV. When she felt the heat beneath the fabric, her hand lingered on a strong shoulder.

"It's been longer than I care to admit since I made out with anyone in a car," Michelle said, her voice hoarse. She pointed at her house. "Want to come in for a while?"

"I'd better not," Amanda said. "I need to call Kathryn, my agent, bright and early tomorrow morning to find out when the producers want to meet me."

Michelle nodded and gently touched Amanda's cheek. "It's a great role. Congratulations again."

"Thanks," Amanda said, suddenly at a loss for words around Michelle.

"I still don't have your number, so you'll need to call me. I don't know if you noticed, but we haven't gotten around to talking about our Valentine's Day date." With the eye that didn't have the scar, Michelle winked at her. "Guess we'll have to meet again to talk about it."

Amanda laughed. "Guess so." She reached past Michelle to open the glove compartment. Her eyes fluttered shut as she breathed in Michelle's scent, and she took longer than necessary to straighten. She took a pen and scribbled her private phone number and her address on the back of her business card. "Here."

Michelle glanced down at the card Amanda handed her. A grin spread over her face. "I've got your number now."

"Oh, you definitely do," Amanda said. Waves of heat still rolled through her body.

After one last kiss that almost made Amanda change her mind about not coming in, Michelle pocketed the card, said goodnight, and got out of the car.

Amanda sat in the driveway and watched her easy, confident stride. It didn't matter anymore that she'd never before been attracted to a butch woman, not when Michelle made her blood boil with a simple touch or a single look.

At the door, Michelle turned and raised her hand.

Amanda waved.

Neither of them moved for several seconds; they just looked at each other from across the driveway. Then, with a glance at the clock on the dashboard, Amanda started the car and pulled out of the driveway after one last wave.

On her way home, she found herself singing along with a love song on the radio, as giddy about their next non-date date as she was about her new role in that crime show.

CHAPTER 5

"Guess where I am?" Amanda asked as she drove through the studio gate and parked her car.

Her grandmother's chuckle echoed through the headset. "Still with your yummy photographer?"

"She's not *my* photographer," Amanda said but couldn't deny that she found Michelle yummy too. The memory of their kisses still made her tingle all over. "And I'm not with Michelle."

Silence filled the line for a few moments.

"Having to climb behind my TV stand in her dating clothes didn't scare her off, did it?" her grandmother asked, sounding worried.

"No. She's not the type to be afraid of a little dust—or a meddling grandmother."

"Meddling? Me?" When Amanda said nothing, her grandmother sighed and dropped the innocent act. "I didn't mean to be an overprotective grandmother hen, but after talking you into calling her, I wanted to make sure she's suitable dating material."

"And?" Amanda asked before she could stop herself. "Is she?" Right now, she should be focusing on her new role—the chance of a lifetime—not on a relationship that might not work out, but still she held her breath as she waited for her grandmother's reply.

"Well, let's just say if I were fifty years younger..."

"You'd still be straight."

"I kissed a woman once," her grandmother said, as if it were a badge of honor.

Amanda rolled her eyes. "It was a film kiss, Grandma."

"Everyone said I was quite convincing."

"You were. I just hope I'll be half as convincing in my new role." That thought reminded her of where she was and started the nervous churning of her stomach again.

"Bah. Being eaten by a giant lizard doesn't take much finesse. You could play that role in your sleep. Don't worry."

True, but playing a detective with a gambling addiction was much more challenging. The script for her character's first episode had arrived by messenger at six o'clock this morning, and she was supposed to be in wardrobe and then makeup at eight and in front of the camera at nine.

After more than four years of no progress in her career, everything was moving at a startling pace, and Amanda just hoped that she could keep up. Almost afraid to jinx it, she took a deep breath before she said, "I'm talking about a different role. Have you seen *Central Precinct*?"

Her grandmother let out an unladylike snort. "Does Meg Ryan use Botox?"

Amanda grinned. "I forgot I was talking to the biggest crime show junkie since...well, ever. They just lost their female lead mid-season, and—"

"Jennifer Carson quit?" Her grandmother huffed. "That girl doesn't have the sense God gave a bowl of soggy cornflakes. I can't believe it. Who leaves a show like that? It could have made her career. But then again, she was never very believable as a detective. Did you see the shoes she's wearing on the show? Who would believe she can chase down criminals on three-inch heels?"

"Um, I wouldn't." Amanda made a mental note to wear sensible shoes on set. Crime show fans like her grandmother apparently noticed details like that. So much to think of. Her head was spinning already, and she hadn't even stepped in front of a camera yet.

"See? Whoever they get to replace her should—"

"They want me to replace her."

Her grandmother's rambling stopped immediately. "Oh, honey, that's wonderful. Congratulations. I'm so happy for you." The background noises sounded as if she was doing a victory dance. After a few seconds, she stopped and said, "You never told me you auditioned for that role."

"I didn't."

"You didn't have to audition? They gave you the role without you having to read for it? That's like marrying someone without having had sex first."

"Lalalala. I can't hear you." Amanda covered her ears, however ineffective that was, since she was wearing a headset.

Another car parked next to hers, and a curvy brunette got out.

Amanda did a double-take when she realized that it was Lorena Gonzales, who had won an Emmy for her role as the show's medical examiner. Suddenly, she was glad that she was still sitting in the car, since her knees went weak. "I have to go, Grandma. Wish me luck."

"You won't need it. You've got talent instead."

Holding on to her grandmother's words as if they were a lifeline, Amanda ended the call, wrapped her damp fingers around her copy of the script, and got out of the car.

Next to her, Lorena Gonzales climbed out of her convertible and gave her a friendly smile. "Hi. You're the new detective, right? I mean…you play Linda Halliday."

"Uh, yes. Amanda Clark."

"Lorena Gonzales," Lorena said unnecessarily.

How surreal. From watching Lorena on TV, Amanda was already familiar with her face and her voice, but, of course, they were complete strangers.

They shook hands, and Amanda hoped her palm wasn't too damp.

"Is this your first time on a TV show?" Lorena asked.

Amanda nodded. "I had a few walk-ons in daily soaps, but nothing like this."

"Then you'd better enjoy today, because there's an old saying: The most exciting day of your life is the first day on a set. The most boring day of your life is your second day on a set."

Amanda's heart was racing, and she seriously doubted that she would get bored anytime soon.

At the doubtful expression on her face, Lorena smiled. "Come on. I'll show you the way to the makeup trailer."

After enduring the attentions of some sadist posing as a hair stylist and studying her lines one last time while the makeup artist applied the thick stage makeup, Amanda finally made her way over to the soundstage that Lorena had pointed out earlier.

A large factory with several warehouses had been converted into a studio. The set of *Central Precinct*, designed to look like a police station with one of the walls missing, was a barely controlled chaos. Two technicians climbed on ladders to position the lights; stagehands rearranged a desk and a file cabinet, and production assistants shouted into their walkie-talkies.

The bearded man in the faded jeans had to be Walt Bishop, the director for most of the show's episodes. He was talking to Lorena Gonzales and two other co-stars that Amanda had so far seen only on TV. She couldn't help feeling like a starstruck teenager. Clearly, this was a far cry from the tampon commercials she usually did.

After straightening her shoulders, she stepped over the cables on the floor and joined them. "Mr. Bishop? Amanda Clark."

The director turned. His gaze swept her face and then down her body, taking in the detective clothes wardrobe had given her.

Amanda fidgeted in the chocolate-colored leather jacket. It wasn't her usual style, but she imagined it would have looked great on Michelle. *Stop thinking about her and focus on your job!*

After a second, the director gave her an approving nod and introduced himself.

The man next to him, the epitome of the tall, dark, and handsome actor, grinned at her. "Hey there. I'm Nick Hagan, your new partner. In the completely non-sexual cop sense, of course."

Was this his way of trying to break the ice with the new cast mate, or was he flirting? Well, if he was, he would soon realize that he was barking up the wrong tree. "Of course." Amanda shook his hand too.

Walt waved to his assistant director. "Now that everyone's here, let's do a read-through of today's scenes and then get this show on the road. We've got a murder to solve, people!"

Fourteen long hours later, Amanda was ready to commit murder instead of solving one on TV. It took all of her acting skills to hide how miserable she felt. Her feet ached; she was sweating beneath the hot lights, and she was so hungry that her stomach was probably close to digesting her intestines.

Shooting a TV show clearly wasn't as glamorous as she had expected. Most of her day had consisted of endless repetitions. Sometimes, one of the props had been in the wrong position, the sound guys had angled the boom so that it was visible on screen, or Nick, who played the male lead detective, couldn't remember his lines, so they had to shoot the scene again.

Between takes came the waiting—waiting for makeup to be reapplied, for the cameras to be repositioned, or for the director to instruct one of the actors.

"The next shot after this one will be a martini," Walt finally said.

Amanda breathed a sigh of relief.

"Let's try to get this one in one take," Lorena said. "I want to get out of here before midnight."

So at least she wasn't the only one longing for this day to be over. Amanda took her mark and waited for the by now familiar cadence of shouts.

"Roll sound," the assistant director called.

"Speed," the sound technician answered from behind his mixing board.

"Roll camera."

"Speed."

"Marker," the assistant director called.

The second assistant camera operator stepped in front of the camera with a clapperboard. "Scene twenty-four, take one." He raised the hinged top slat, brought it down with a loud crack, and ducked out of the frame.

Amanda let herself sink into her detective persona as she waited for the director's "action." When it came, she slowly turned and regarded the medical examiner across the stainless steel table. "What did you just say?"

"I said I saw you, Detective. I know you were gambling."

With the same coolness that had allowed Amanda to work with Lizzy after finding her in bed with their co-producer, she narrowed her eyes at the medical examiner. "What I do or don't do in my free time is none of your—"

The ringing of a phone stopped her midline.

"Cut!" the director shouted.

Amanda gritted her teeth. What kind of idiot didn't turn off their cell phone during shooting?

The phone continued to ring, and her colleagues sent each other accusing glances, but no one moved to turn it off.

"I think that's yours." Lorena pointed at Amanda's purse that hung across the back of her folding chair.

Oh, shit. I'm the idiot. "I'm so, so sorry. I thought I'd turned it off." Amanda hurried over and hastily rummaged through her purse to find the offending phone. As she shut it off, she caught a glimpse of the caller ID.

Michelle.

Despite her tension, she couldn't help smiling as she walked back into the fake morgue.

Lorena nudged her and grinned. "You got a hot date with the boyfriend after this?"

Cheeks glowing, Amanda shook her head but said nothing else, not sure if it was a good idea to tell her colleagues she was gay. She didn't want anything to interfere with this once-in-a-lifetime opportunity.

"Let's do this again, people," Walt called. "From 'I said I saw you, Detective.'"

Amanda shut away all thoughts of Michelle and focused on her job.

Amanda sank into the driver's seat of her car and moaned in delight at how good it felt to be off her feet. She sat there for a minute without starting the car, her head still buzzing with everything she had experienced that day. Finally, she dug her cell phone out of her purse and turned it back on. She was bursting to tell someone of her first day on the set of *Central Precinct*.

The reminder of the missed call from earlier flashed across the screen, and she pressed the button to call Michelle back.

Michelle picked up on the first ring, as if she had been hovering next to the phone. "Hi, Amanda," she said, her warm voice wrapping around Amanda like a cuddly blanket. "How are you doing? Have you heard from the TV show people?"

A car honked next to her, and Lorena Gonzales waved as she pulled out of the parking lot.

"Heard from them? I spent the last fifteen hours in front of the camera."

"Wow. They don't waste any time, do they?"

Amanda shrugged. "Time is money, especially in show biz."

"So how was it?" Michelle asked, sounding genuinely interested.

For once, Amanda struggled to find the right words. "Exciting, boring, exhausting, wonderful, scary."

Michelle laughed, not the tittering, polite laugh that Amanda had heard all day from some of the actresses, but a deep belly laugh that made her smile. "All of that and a bag of cookies, huh?"

"No cookies on set, I'm afraid." As if on cue, Amanda's stomach growled.

"Have you eaten?"

"No. I only had time to grab a turkey sub from the catering table at lunch."

Another car honked as more of her co-stars left for the day.

"Where are you?" Michelle asked.

Amanda rubbed her face, a bit embarrassed to admit it. "Still in the studio's parking lot."

"Want to come over? I could cook something for you."

Part of Amanda longed to spend some time with Michelle, and her stomach rejoiced at the offer of food, but she knew it wasn't a good idea. "I can't. It's late, and I have to be back on set at six tomorrow morning, so I'd better get myself home."

"Tomorrow? They're shooting on a Sunday?"

"They lost a few days while the decision to sign me as the new lead was made, so now everyone has to work overtime to make up for it." Amanda didn't mind, except for the fact that it meant she wouldn't get to see Michelle anytime soon.

"Damn. Hollywood sure doesn't keep regular hours. Please eat something before you go to bed, okay?"

No one but her grandmother had ever worried about whether she was eating enough. Amanda decided that she liked having someone care enough to worry. "I'll toss together something quick," she said and found herself reluctant to end the call.

Michelle was silent, as if she didn't want to say goodbye either. "Drive carefully," she finally said.

"I will. Goodnight."

"Goodnight. Oh, and Amanda?"

The way Michelle said her name made goose bumps erupt all over Amanda's body. "Yeah?"

"Knock 'em dead tomorrow."

Laughing, Amanda hung up and started the car.

At four thirty, Amanda stumbled from the bathroom into her tiny kitchen and stared bleary-eyed into her fridge. She pushed a wilted salad and a nearly empty jar of mayonnaise out of the way and sniffed two-day-old Chinese takeout. "Ugh."

Just as she closed the fridge empty-handedly and turned toward the coffeepot, the doorbell rang.

She nearly jumped out of her skin, the adrenaline kick helping to wake her up. Grumbling, she walked over to the intercom. Who the hell was ringing her doorbell at this ungodly hour? *Please, please, please, don't let it be a messenger with a script change.*

She had stayed up, memorizing her lines, until one o'clock, but her colleagues had warned her that the script for the day could change at any time. Warily, she pressed the button to talk to whoever was on her doorstep. "Yes?"

"Uh, it's me. Michelle. I hope I didn't wake you."

Amanda stared at the intercom. "What are you doing here?"

"Bringing you breakfast."

Amanda continued to stare. Michelle had gotten up in the middle of the night and driven over all the way from the Hollywood Hills just to bring her breakfast?

"I'm sorry," Michelle said when Amanda stayed silent. "Maybe this wasn't such a great idea after all. I'd better go."

Belatedly, Amanda pressed the buzzer. "No, please. Come up. Top floor."

"If you're sure..."

"I'm sure. Now hurry up and feed me, woman."

Chuckles echoed through the intercom, followed by the sound of the building's front door closing behind Michelle.

Amanda bounced on the balls of her feet as she waited for the elevator to make it to her floor. She threw a quick glance at her image in the mirror and ran her hands through her hair. She hadn't applied any makeup, knowing the makeup artist would just wash it off and begin anew anyway. Now she hoped the signs of just three hours of sleep weren't too noticeable.

When the elevator announced Michelle's arrival, she removed the chain and opened the door.

Michelle stood in front of her in jeans and a leather jacket, loaded down by various bowls and a thermos, her hair disheveled.

The urge to just pull her into the apartment and kiss her surprised Amanda. Instead, she just stood and stared.

"Top floor, huh?" Michelle said, shuffling her feet.

"Yeah. I even have an ocean view." Amanda realized she was blocking the doorway and hastily stepped aside. "Come on in. The kitchen's over there."

Michelle squeezed past her in the narrow hall, and Amanda greedily inhaled her scent of night air, leather, and men's cologne. That combination had never smelled so good on anyone else.

"How long until you have to leave for work?" Michelle asked.

Amanda glanced at her wristwatch. This early, LA's streets wouldn't be as congested, but it would still take her almost an hour to get to the studio. "About thirty minutes."

"Good." Michelle entered the kitchen, put down the bowls she had brought, and shrugged out of her leather jacket. "Frying pan?"

"Uh. Here." Amanda stepped closer and leaned around Michelle to get the pan out of the cabinet. Another whiff of Michelle's cologne made her head spin, and she clutched Michelle's shoulder to keep her balance.

"Careful." Michelle held on to her hips with both hands and pulled her closer as if to steady her with her own body.

Heat sizzled between them. Amanda's gaze darted from Michelle's eyes to her mouth. With a groan, she gave in and did what she'd wanted to do from the moment Michelle had shown up on her doorstep. She wrapped her arms around her and kissed her.

Moaning, Michelle surged against her and returned the kiss. She nibbled, teased, and stroked with her teeth, lips, and tongue until Amanda nearly sank to the kitchen floor.

By the time they separated, they were both gasping for air.

Still clutching Michelle's shoulders, Amanda whispered against her lips, "Oh God, that was…"

"Yeah. It sure was." Michelle took the forgotten frying pan out of Amanda's limp grasp. "You." She pointed. "Out of the kitchen. You're too distracting."

After stealing one last kiss, Amanda lifted her hands and retreated to the doorway. From there, she watched Michelle work at the stove. Soon heavenly scents drifted through her kitchen, but despite her growling stomach, Amanda was more interested in admiring Michelle's ass. She had to admit that she was developing a healthy appreciation for a woman in jeans. This woman in jeans, at least.

"Get ready to sit down. Banana pancakes in two minutes. Where do you keep the—?" Michelle turned and caught her staring. "What?"

Amanda said the first thing that came to mind. "You're too good to be true."

"No, I'm not. You work hard, so you deserve to be spoiled a little. Plates?"

Amanda walked over and reached around her for the plates, this time careful to keep some distance between their bodies. If she got lost in Michelle's kisses again, she'd never make it to work on time.

Michelle chuckled as if she knew what Amanda was doing. She took the plates from her and pointed at the small table in the breakfast nook. "Sit. I'll bring the pancakes over in a minute."

Obediently, Amanda sat. The script was still lying on the table, where she'd left it last night, and she flipped it open to study her lines one last time while she waited for breakfast to be served.

Halfway down the first page of the script, a startled cry from Michelle made her look up in alarm.

"Uh, Amanda? Your roommate is trying to climb my body."

Probably lured in by the sounds of food being prepared in the kitchen, Mischief had gotten up from his place at the bottom of her bed and was now climbing Michelle's body as if she were a tree.

Not that Amanda could blame him. She'd had the same impulse just a few minutes earlier. But, of course, that didn't mean she'd let him pierce Michelle with his needle-sharp claws. "Mischief! Get down!"

Naturally, the cat scrambled even higher up Michelle's body.

Amanda strode over, plucked him off, and set him back on the floor. "You'd better stay down there, Mister!"

Michelle rubbed her thighs. "Ouch."

"Are you okay?"

"Yeah. I'm fine. It just hurt for a second when he dug his claws in."

Amanda resisted the urge to run her hands over Michelle and make sure she was really fine. After all, it was a bit early in their relationship to tell Michelle to pull down her pants.

Keeping an eye on Mischief's claws, Michelle bent and scratched him behind one ear. "I can see why you named him Mischief."

"I didn't. He already had that name when I met him at a commercial shoot for cat food. He was doing his name proud, getting into all kinds of mischief, holding up the shooting for three hours. The animal trainer was ready to have him put down, and my fellow actor was quite willing to do it right then and there."

"And you?"

"Well, I wasn't exactly amused either. I lost my job as a waitress that night because I didn't show up for work on time." If not for her grandmother, she would have starved to death that month because she'd been too proud to ask her parents for money to tide her over until she found the job at the juice bar. "But just because Mischief obviously wasn't cut out to be an actor, I couldn't let them harm him, so I talked them into letting me take him home."

Michelle smiled, stepped closer, and kissed Amanda's cheek in a gesture so tender that it nearly made Amanda melt into a puddle on her kitchen floor. "Maybe you're the one who's too good to be true."

They stared into each other's eyes until Michelle whirled around to the stove. "Oh, shit. The pancakes." She slid them onto the plates and sprinkled some cinnamon on top. "Sit."

The scent of cinnamon, bananas, and Michelle lured Amanda back to the table.

Mischief followed them but quickly lost interest when he realized they were having only pancakes, no bacon, so he stalked back to the bedroom.

Michelle pulled a chair out for Amanda and placed one plate in front of her. "Bon appétit." She sat across from her, but instead of eating, she watched Amanda dig into her pancake.

"Oh God," Amanda moaned for the second time this morning. "These are incredible. Aren't you having any?"

A smile crinkled the scar at the corner of Michelle's eye. "I'm too busy enjoying the view."

Amanda's cheeks heated. "There's nothing attractive about me wolfing down my breakfast."

Michelle just smiled. "Let me be the judge of that."

Not sure what to answer, Amanda took another bite of pancake. Finally, after she had finished off not only her own pancake but also Michelle's, she carried the plates to the sink. "I'm sorry I don't have time to give you the nickel tour of the apartment or to show you my ocean view," she said over her shoulder.

"Next time. That is if you want me to come over again."

Their gazes met from across the room.

"I do," Amanda said and realized that it sounded like a much bigger commitment than just seeing each other again. A few days ago, that would have scared her, but being with Michelle felt just right. She would follow her grandmother's advice and at least give this a chance to see where it was going.

At exactly five o'clock, Amanda was out the door with a full belly, a thermos of coffee, and one last, thorough kiss. She hoped the makeup artist had something in her bag to help conceal her kiss-swollen lips—otherwise, Detective Linda Halliday would look as if she had been kissed long and hard by someone who knew what she was doing.

CHAPTER 6

WHEN AMANDA SAW THE NAME on her cell's display, she was glad that she had decided to pick up her phone. Because of her six-days-a-week shooting schedule, she hadn't seen Michelle since their four-a.m. breakfast almost three weeks ago, and to her surprise, she'd found that she missed her. She covered one ear with her free hand to block out the noise in the background. "Hi, Michelle."

"Hi, you. Are you lazing around in bed?"

Amanda looked at the gathered crowd in the studio's parking lot and the big red sign she had been holding up before her cell phone had started ringing. It said, "When you play me, pay me." No, this definitely didn't look like her peaceful bedroom. "Uh, no, why?"

"My sources in show biz tell me the actors are on strike."

"You have sources in show biz?"

"This is LA." Michelle chuckled. "Everyone has sources in show biz. So, did I hear right?"

Amanda nodded, even though Michelle couldn't see it. "You did. The SAG went on strike this morning."

Cheers and shouts rose around Amanda as a handful of A-list actors joined the picket lines.

"Uh, obviously you're not using your day off to sleep in," Michelle said. "Where are you?"

"In front of the biggest studio in Hollywood."

"You're supporting the strike?" Michelle sounded surprised. "Excuse me for saying so, but I would have thought since you joined the cast of *Central Precinct*, you make a more than reasonable living."

Amanda certainly had no reason for complaints in that area, and frankly, she wasn't too happy about the strike holding up their spring season, but she wanted to show her solidarity with her less fortunate colleagues. "I do," she said. "But I haven't forgotten what it's like to live hand to mouth, like most actors."

Michelle was silent for a moment. "That's a great thing you're doing."

Amanda shrugged. "Nothing much. But if we keep this up, I hope the big studios will listen."

"Want some support? I could come over, wave a few signs around, or take photos if it's needed."

Holding back an immediate "yes," Amanda asked instead, "Don't you have to work?"

"I do, but... Well, I could go on strike too."

"Uh, you work for yourself."

"Yeah, what can I say? The boss is a tyrant."

Amanda laughed. "I don't believe that for a second. She's a real teddy bear."

"Teddy bear?" Michelle growled. "Don't let that get around, or you'll ruin my reputation."

"Don't worry. Your secret is safe with me."

They were both silent for a moment before Michelle asked, "So, how about it? Should I go on strike too?"

"You don't have to do that. Basically, we're just standing around, gossiping about the latest Hollywood rumors. You'd just get bored."

"Not as long as you're there," Michelle said.

Again, her openness made Amanda speechless.

"Okay, if you don't want me to join you, how about going out on a da—uh, I mean, doing a little rehearsal with me later?" Michelle asked after a few seconds of silence. "Or would that be considered breaking the picket lines?"

Amanda smiled. "No, I'm sure a little rehearsal would be fine."

"Great. Then how about I pick you up at seven and we go to that Mexican restaurant we went to last time?"

"Uh..." Amanda didn't want to risk having that same impolite waiter again. "Seven is fine, but how about that little Italian restaurant on Hillhurst Avenue instead?"

"That's good too. I look forward to it."

"Me too."

"Hey, Amanda," Lorena called from a few yards away. "Stop flirting with your boyfriend and start holding up that sign!"

"Yeah, yeah, yeah. Hold your horses." To Michelle, she said, "I have to go. The Hollywood diva next to me is getting impatient."

"I heard that!" Lorena shouted.

Amanda laughed. During the last few weeks, she had gotten friendly with most of her co-stars, especially Lorena.

"Until later," Michelle said. "Have fun gossiping."

"Will do." Smiling in anticipation, Amanda ended the call and picked up the sign.

"Uh, I'm sure the restaurant will have something to drink available," Michelle said when Amanda climbed into the passenger seat of the SUV, balancing a tray of plastic cups.

Amanda chuckled. "It's not for me. Do you mind if we take a bit of a detour? I wanted to deliver this earlier, but I was running late."

"No problem." Michelle closed the door for Amanda and got in on the driver's side. "So, where to, milady?"

Amanda gave her the address.

"Oh, you want to look in on your grandmother?"

"Not just her. The neighbors too. The juice is for them."

Michelle arched one eyebrow. She looked away from the street to throw a quick glance at the transparent cups. "You're delivering juice to your grandmother's neighbors?"

"They're a couple of nice elderly ladies she plays bridge with every Tuesday," Amanda said and then realized that didn't explain anything. "When I started working at the juice bar, I got into the habit of bringing them some juice every time I visited my grandmother."

"But you don't work there anymore."

Amanda shrugged. "They don't know that." And she wasn't about to tell them. She had even sworn her grandmother to secrecy.

"I don't understand."

"They don't have much money, but they're too proud to accept a little charity. I want them to have some vitamins, so I'm letting them think I get the juice for free because I work at the juice bar."

"Oh, wow. That's sneaky. And very nice of you."

Amanda doffed an imaginary hat. "I got it from my grandmother."

"What? Being sneaky or being nice?"

Stealing Michelle's signature gesture, Amanda winked at her. "Both."

"So," Amanda said when they lingered over desserts. "Tell me a little about your ex, the actress."

Michelle scooped whipped cream onto her spoon. "Which one?"

"Oh, right, you said there were two."

"Yes. Though one was a stage actress."

Amanda licked a crumb of cheesecake off her fork. "And the other one?"

"Mostly small roles in TV movies, but she thought she was the next Jodie Foster, Angelina Jolie, and Marilyn Monroe all rolled into one."

That didn't sound like anyone the down-to-earth Michelle would keep company with, much less be involved with romantically. "How did you meet?"

Michelle pushed back her homemade Italian ice cream as if she'd lost her appetite. "That was during my short stint as a paparazza."

Amanda couldn't help staring. "You were a paparazza?" She couldn't imagine the gentle, honest Michelle as one of the celebrity-chasing press sharks.

"Just for a few weeks. I'm not proud of it, but I was struggling to get my studio off the ground and…"

Amanda reached across the table and covered Michelle's hand with her own. "I understand."

Michelle looked up. "Do you?"

"You wouldn't believe some of the jobs I did to support myself while I auditioned for bit roles and commercials."

"Oh, yeah?"

"Yeah. But we're not talking about my embarrassing time as a nude model for an art class. We were talking about your ex."

Michelle's gaze went hazy. "Uh, you do know that photographers have excellent visual imagination, don't you? And you just gave mine one hell of a workout."

Amanda ignored the comment and her own blush. "Your ex," she reminded.

"Right. Well, not much to tell. I was young and stupid, just looking for a beautiful face and a hot body instead of the things that really count, so I asked her out—and she said yes. We were together for eleven turbulent months; then I found out she was cheating on me while she was on location." Michelle grimaced. "When I confronted her, all she had to say was that whatever happened on location didn't mean a thing. It was an actor thing that I, as a mere mortal, just couldn't understand."

Amanda knew some actors who thought like that. Hell, it turned out that a few of her exes had shared that kind of attitude, but Amanda had never understood it. Suddenly, making sure Michelle didn't lump her in with that sort of actress was important to her. "Bullshit."

A grin spread over Michelle's face. "Bullshit?"

"Yeah, that's complete and utter bullshit. I'm not saying I'm much better than your ex at relationships, but—"

"Really? So far, I don't have any complaints." Michelle took Amanda's free hand and kissed it.

Did Michelle really classify what they had as a relationship already? *Oh, and you don't?* If she was honest with herself, she hadn't even looked at other women since Valentine's Day. She cleared her throat. "Wait until I forget your birthday because I'm busy trying to land a role. Or call you by the name of the love interest in the movie I'm auditioning for."

"Ouch. You did all that in a past relationship?"

Amanda pressed her lips together and nodded. "Yes. I never, ever cheated on anyone, but otherwise, I sure don't deserve an award for girlfriend of the year." Fiddling with her fork, she glanced across the table at Michelle and gathered the courage to ask what had been on her mind a lot in the past weeks. "So I don't get why you're so intent on dating me, especially since you swore to never get involved with another actress. What made you give up that resolution? I'm sure it wasn't my charming, hungover self on the morning after we first met." God, she'd been such an ungrateful, judgmental bitch.

Michelle smiled. "Yeah, I have to admit you certainly came across like the high-maintenance diva type. A hot diva type, but still. I didn't know whether to be amused or insulted at your assumptions about butches."

Amanda pinched the bridge of her nose. "I'm so sorry. I feel stupid about it now, but I just... I don't know. Maybe I am a high-maintenance diva after all. I guess I've been in the business for too long, surrounded by all the Hollywood standards of how a woman should look and behave. It's not an excuse, but..."

"It's okay. Water under the bridge," Michelle said, sounding as if she meant it.

Amanda sent her a grateful smile. "What made you want to date me anyway? Is it because I look like my grandmother? I know you had a crush on her when you were a little girl, and they say that the first crush is the deepest, so—"

Michelle reached across the table and stopped her rambling with a soft touch to her lips. "I admit when I first saw you, it was your resemblance to Josephine that caught my attention, but that alone wouldn't have made me give up my resolution to stay the hell away from actresses."

Amanda had no reason not to believe her. So far, Michelle had always been honest and up-front with her. "What was it, then?"

"Your grandmother." She held up a hand before Amanda could interrupt. "Not the way you think. When we watched that movie, *Spur of the Moment,* and whenever you talked about her, I could tell how much she means to you. We have that in common. Our love for our grandparents, I mean. That's what made me take a second look at you."

"And you liked what you saw?" It was still hard for Amanda to believe when she thought about that morning after Valentine's Day.

"Oh, yeah. That first morning, you were so confused and mortally embarrassed about waking up in my bed. I could tell you're not a partying starlet who drinks too much and falls into bed with some stranger on a regular basis."

Amanda shook her head. "I have never done that in my life."

"I liked that. I like that you're not a typical actress. My exes, Elizabeth and Jessica, couldn't read the newspaper without throwing a temper tantrum if they weren't in it. They wanted to go to every party and hang out with the cool people. You, however, read the newspaper for the news and the crossword puzzle, hang out with your grandmother, rescue cats that make you get fired, go on strike to support your colleagues, and buy juice for elderly people." Michelle looked at her with a tender smile. "Right from the start, you didn't fit my image of an actress at all. A photographer is supposed to see beneath the surface and look at what's really there, and I realized I hadn't been doing that. I was stereotyping based on my limited experiences with two actresses, convincing myself that I needed to stay away because all actresses are like that."

So, basically, they were both guilty of the same thing—stereotyping. But Amanda had to admit that it had taken her a bit longer to give up her preconceived notions about butch women. She shook her head at herself. "We're a fine pair, aren't we?"

A soft smile curved Michelle's lips. "I happen to think so, yes."

"Amanda?" Someone stopped next to their table. "Hi. I thought that was you."

Amanda felt herself blanch. *Damn. Speaking of exes...* "Hello, Lizzy," she said, not even trying to fake a friendly smile. "What do you want? Did you get bored with your co-producer already?"

Lizzy clutched her chest. "No reason to be that way. I just came over to congratulate you on your new role. You look good on TV. Although..." She leaned closer. "Whenever they do close-ups, you can see a few wrinkles here and here and especially here." She touched Amanda's forehead, cheek, and the corner of her eye.

The touch made Amanda shiver, and it wasn't in a pleasant way. Barely resisting the urge to slap Lizzy's hand away, she scooted her chair back to escape the close proximity.

Lizzy still pretended to study her face. "You're over thirty, dear. Maybe it's time to get some work done. And why don't you think about getting a boob job while you're at it?"

Amanda forced herself not to react and pasted on a stoic expression, not wanting to give Lizzy the satisfaction of getting a rise out of her.

Michelle put down her spoon with a clank, drawing Lizzy's attention toward her for the first time. "You'd know all about that, wouldn't you? Wrinkles and getting some work done."

Lizzy's eyes widened almost comically. "You...?" She stared at Michelle and then looked back and forth between her and Amanda. "Don't tell me you two are...? I didn't know you went for her type." She made a face as if she'd just smelled something foul and pointed with her thumb at Michelle.

"What's that supposed to mean?" Amanda asked, not sure why she was even bothering to talk to Lizzy.

"Oh, nothing." Lizzy gave her a sugary-sweet grin. "Just that I thought you preferred a real woman in bed."

The heat of anger shot up Amanda's neck. She jumped up, her dessert fork raised as if it were a dagger. "Enough!" Lizzy could bad-mouth her all she wanted, but Michelle was off limits. "Michelle is more of a woman than you could ever be."

"Oh, I know for a fact that she—"

"Shut up!" Amanda's ears started to buzz.

Before she could lose control, a hand closed around her fist clutching the fork. "She's not worth it, Amanda," Michelle said from behind her.

Amanda took a deep breath, startled at how strongly she had reacted. With the exception of her grandmother, she had never felt so protective of anyone in her life.

One of the waiters hurried over. "Is everything all right, ladies?"

Without looking away from her stare-down with Lizzy, Amanda nodded. "Everything's fine. She was just leaving."

Huffing, Lizzy lifted her head up high and marched away.

As soon as she was out of sight, Amanda sank back onto her chair and covered her face with one of her hands. Why did each of their dates—or rather their rehearsals—have to end with some kind of disaster? "I'm so sorry. Like you probably guessed, that was—"

"Lizzy Wade, your ex."

Amanda looked up. "You know her?"

Michelle plopped down onto her chair, her face unusually pale beneath her tan. "Sadly, I do. In the biblical sense. Elizabeth is my ex too."

"What?" The fork clattered onto her plate. "Are you serious?"

"As a heart attack."

Amanda massaged her temples with both hands. "No wonder you didn't want anything to do with actresses anymore." She shook herself. "God, we slept with the same woman. That's...ugh."

"Yeah." Michelle grimaced. "Who knew we both go for the same type of woman?"

"Not anymore," Amanda muttered. "I'm changing my type."

The frown on Michelle's face slowly disappeared and was replaced by a smile. "Oh? So what's your type now?"

"I'm favoring the honest, monogamous, butch type."

"Hmm." Michelle rubbed her chin as if considering each item on Amanda's list. "If I know a woman fitting that description, should I give her your number?"

"No."

Michelle's gaze darted to Amanda's eyes. "No?" she asked, a hint of a tremor in her voice.

"No," Amanda repeated. "That won't be necessary. She's already got my number."

The smile made its way back onto Michelle's face. "Oh, she does?" she drawled.

The seductive purr made Amanda shiver, and this time, it was the pleasant kind. "Yes, she does." She raised her hand to summon the waiter, who hovered nearby. "Come on. Let's get out of here. After that woman touched me, I need a hot shower, a facial scrub, and a shot of something strong, not necessarily in that order."

"Can I come?" Michelle asked.

Amanda wagged her finger at her. "For the hot shower? Nice try."

"I wouldn't say no to sharing a shower with you, but I was talking about the shot of something strong." Michelle grinned. "Because the last time you were drinking, you ended up in my bed."

The waiter cleared his throat next to them.

A blush heated Amanda's cheeks. *Great. Another waiter with perfect timing.* She forced a smile and peered up at him. "It's not like it sounds."

"Of course not, ma'am," the waiter said and almost kept a straight face.

"It's not!"

Laughing, Michelle handed him a few bills, said, "Keep the rest," and pulled Amanda out of the restaurant.

Michelle found an empty spot on the street in front of Amanda's apartment building, parked the car, and turned off the engine. "So..."

"So," Amanda repeated.

"Thanks for a wonderful evening," Michelle said.

Amanda had enjoyed the evening too, and she didn't want it to end. "Thank you for inviting me."

Silence spread through the car until Michelle said, "I'll walk you to the door." She got out and walked around to open the passenger-side door for Amanda.

As she climbed out of the SUV, their bodies brushed, sending tingles through Amanda.

Michelle turned around and pressed a button on her key to lock the car and then placed her hand in the small of Amanda's back as they walked toward the front door.

The heat of her palm seared through the fabric of Amanda's blouse.

They climbed the front steps of the apartment building and stopped at the door. Amanda fumbled for her keys in her purse and unlocked the front door but then paused in the doorway. "Do you want to come up for that shot of something strong?"

Michelle studied her as if trying to find out whether she was being invited in for a drink or something more.

Amanda wasn't so sure of the answer herself. The pull between them was strong—so strong that it almost scared her a little. Most of her past relationships had been pleasant, but they had never made her wish the strike would go on indefinitely so that she could hole up in bed with her lover.

Michelle glanced at the door and then at Amanda. She swallowed audibly. "I very much want to come up, but not for a shot of something strong." Her heated gaze felt like a caress. "That's why I should go."

But instead of turning and walking away, they both stood on the top step, staring at each other.

Finally, Michelle cleared her throat. "Goodnight." She bent and kissed Amanda on the lips. It was tender and careful, as if she was keeping her passion leashed.

Oh, no. Something inside of Amanda instantly wanted to break through that chivalrous self-control—so she did. Before Michelle could step back, Amanda slid her fingers into her short hair, pulled her closer, and deepened the kiss. "Maybe I don't want you to go," she whispered against Michelle's lips.

"Maybe?" Michelle whispered back.

Instead of an answer, Amanda reached for her hand and pulled her into the building and over to the elevator. It seemed to take forever for the doors to open, but finally they slid apart. Amanda and Michelle stumbled inside.

Amanda's fingers were shaking slightly as she pressed the button for the top floor.

Their gazes met in the mirrored wall.

The instant the doors closed behind them, Michelle pinned her against the wall with her whole body and captured her mouth in a demanding kiss.

Amanda had just a second to be grateful that her elevator didn't have a camera system before she lost all ability to think. Her arms went around Michelle's neck, and she strained against her. God, this woman knew how to kiss.

Michelle braced her hands on either side of Amanda's head as if she needed the support to stay upright. Her tongue traced fiery trails over Amanda's.

Amanda dug her fingers into her shoulders. The railing behind her pressed into her back, and she arched her hips toward Michelle. The answering moan made her quiver.

With a loud ding, the elevator reached the top floor.

Someone cleared his throat only a few feet away.

Michelle's heat disappeared from Amanda's body. Weak-limbed, she leaned against the elevator wall before straightening to face her neighbor, who stood in front of the elevator, staring at them.

With a mumbled greeting, she slipped past him, dragging Michelle with her by the hand.

The neighbor gave them a curious glance as they passed.

The elevator doors whooshed closed, leaving them alone in the hallway.

On legs that still felt unsteady, Amanda stumbled to her apartment door. It took her almost a minute to get the key in the lock. When the door finally opened, she turned and regarded Michelle, who waited behind her, no longer touching her.

Passion made Michelle's brown eyes seem to glow from within, but there were also other emotions written on that expressive face. Desire. Tenderness. Affection. Maybe even love. If she took Michelle into her bedroom now, it would mean more than just a release of the sexual tension between them. Was she ready for that?

"Second thoughts?" Michelle asked, her voice low and hoarse.

Amanda licked her lips. They were tender from their kisses. "What if I said yes?"

Michelle stepped closer, but not close enough for their bodies to touch. She took Amanda's face into her hands and trailed her thumbs over her cheeks. "Then I'd give you a chaste kiss on the cheek and leave."

Amanda smiled. She had no doubt that Michelle would do just that, but a chaste kiss and Michelle leaving weren't what she wanted. She slowly shook her head. "No second thoughts." She pulled Michelle over the doorstep.

The loud ringing of a cell phone made both of them groan.

Cursing, Amanda let go of Michelle's hand to search her purse for the phone. "I'm so sorry. I keep forgetting to turn the damn thing off."

"Uh, no. It's actually mine." Her cheeks tinged red, Michelle fumbled the ringing cell phone from the back pocket of her pants. "What is it, Marty? Now is really not a good ti—"

An urgent male voice started speaking on the other end of the line, but Amanda couldn't understand what he was saying.

"Slow down," Michelle said. "What happened?" When the man answered, her face went pale. "Jesus. Is it bad?"

Frowning, Amanda stepped closer and touched her arm in a gesture of silent support.

Michelle looked up and put her free hand on Amanda's while she listened.

"Yes, sure. I can be there in twenty minutes. No, you don't need to do that. It's not a problem, really. See you." Michelle put the phone back into her pocket and leaned into Amanda for a moment.

Amanda rubbed her back. "What happened?"

"One of my nephews and my youngest niece were fighting over some toy. Jackson crashed into the coffee table. My brother is pretty sure his arm is broken. They need to take him to the ER, and they want me to come over to keep an eye on the rest of the brood."

Gently touching the scar at the corner of Michelle's eye, Amanda said, "Sounds like they're a little too much like you and your brother when you were kids."

A smile darted across Michelle's face, but the worried expression didn't leave her eyes. "Guess so. I'm sorry to have to cut this," she pointed between the two of them, "short. That's not how I wanted this night to end."

"It's okay. Maybe this wasn't meant to happen yet. Waiting a little longer might be a good idea." The attraction was definitely there, but there was still so much she didn't know about Michelle.

Michelle nodded with just a hint of regret on her face. "Yeah. This is worth doing it right."

"Do you want me to come with you?"

Michelle shook her head. "Knowing my nieces and nephews, they'll keep me up most of the night, arguing over who gets to be the first to sign their brother's shiny new cast, and you actresses need your beauty sleep." She lifted one hand and caressed Amanda's cheek. "But I'd love to rehearse with you again if the strike is still going on tomorrow."

"You've got a date."

"A date?"

"Um, a rehearsal, of course."

They walked the few steps back to the elevator hand in hand.

Instead of kissing her goodnight, Michelle pulled her into her arms for an embrace.

Amanda pressed her face against the side of Michelle's neck and held her close for a few moments before letting go.

The elevator doors dinged open.

"Let me know how your nephew is doing," Amanda said.

"I will. Sleep well." One last touch of their fingertips, then the elevator doors closed between them and Michelle was gone.

CHAPTER 7

"How's Vegas?" Michelle asked.

Amanda leaned against the headboard of the hotel bed and pressed the phone to her ear as if that would bring them closer. "Big. Flashy." Mentally, she added, *Lonely*.

She'd been as excited as the rest of the cast when Walt had announced that they were going to Las Vegas to film on location, but after five days, she was really starting to miss Michelle. Talking to her on the phone every night wasn't the same as actually seeing her, even if it had brought them closer, forcing them to talk and get to know each other without the distraction of the physical attraction between them.

"When are you coming home?" Michelle asked as if she was thinking along the same lines.

"Probably on Sunday," Amanda said. "We're filming in one of the big casinos tomorrow. Nick and I are investigating the death of a gambler who was trying to cheat the casino."

Michelle laughed. "Do you realize that you sound like you're really a detective?"

A blush crept up Amanda's neck. Since joining the cast of *Central Precinct* four weeks ago, she'd done little else but eat, sleep, and be in front of the camera, so the lines between her role and reality were beginning to blur. Sometimes, she felt that Michelle was the only thing tethering her to her normal life. "Sorry. What I wanted to say is that my character—"

"It's all right. I won't complain if you come home with a pair of handcuffs in your suitcase."

The seductive tone of her voice made Amanda's heartbeat spike. She rubbed her chest and then stopped when she realized that the touch made her nipples harden. She squeezed her eyes shut and focused on the sound of Michelle's breathing, but that didn't help as images of Michelle gasping for breath, writhing and bucking beneath Amanda's hands, flashed through her mind.

"What are you thinking about?" Michelle asked softly.

"Uh…" Amanda covered her hot face with her free hand. She couldn't tell Michelle what had gone through her mind…could she?

"You know I was only joking about the handcuffs, don't you? I'm not into BDSM."

"Me neither."

Just when Amanda was gathering the courage to ask Michelle what she *was* into, a knock sounded at the door to her hotel room.

"Jesus." Amanda jumped off the bed, not sure if she should be glad or annoyed. "Give me a minute. Someone's at my door. Probably just room service with my dinner." She put down the cell phone and went to open the door.

Instead of room service, her colleague Nick stood in front of her. "Hi. I thought since we wrapped early today, I'd take advantage and get in some sightseeing. Want to come?" He dazzled her with the smile that had won him two Emmys and the attention of countless women.

"Uh…" Amanda pointed over her shoulder to the bed, where her cell phone lay. "I'm on the phone."

Nick made no move to back away. "No problem. I can wait, if you want."

Normally, Amanda would have jumped at the chance to see the sights of Las Vegas, but she didn't want to waste what little time she had with Michelle. Plus she got the feeling that Nick was interested in more than a companion for sightseeing, and she didn't want to send him the wrong message. "Not tonight. All I want is to put up my feet and not think of anything work-related until tomorrow morning."

"I hear you. Maybe another time, then."

Amanda gave a noncommittal half-nod. Once Nick left, she closed the door and walked back to the bed. She got comfortable again and raised the phone to her ear. "Sorry. Just one of my colleagues."

"I heard. Didn't you want to go with him? You're not obliged to talk to me every night, you know?"

"I know. I want to," Amanda said, because it was true. "Besides, sightseeing with Nick might not be the best idea."

"Why not? From what you told me about him, he seems like an okay guy."

"He is, but…" Amanda sighed. "I don't want to sound like a full-of-herself Hollywood starlet, but I have a feeling he's interested in me."

"Oh. Well, I can't blame him."

Shaking her head, Amanda had to smile nonetheless. "Charmer."

"Just stating the facts, ma'am. A few million Americans happen to agree with me."

"What did you do, take out a poll?" Amanda asked with a laugh.

"Not quite, but have you seen the ratings of *Central Precinct*? They've gone up since you joined the cast."

She was right. Amanda had followed the numbers religiously but hesitated to attribute the improved ratings to her presence on the show. "It's the writing. We have some very talented writers on the show. When I first joined the cast, there was this storyline about Detective Halliday's father that—"

"I watched it. It was great writing—and great acting."

Amanda smiled. "Thanks. So you're watching us regularly? Are you a fan of the show?"

"I'm a fan of you," Michelle said. "And I don't mean just of your acting chops."

Once again, Michelle's openness made Amanda speechless. Suddenly, she couldn't wait to be with her again, to talk face-to-face, and to exchange a kiss or two. *Or a few hundred.* "When can I see you?"

"When does your plane land? I'll come pick you up."

"No. We'll take the red-eye and land at two in the morning. That's too late for you to be driving all over LA."

"It's not a problem," Michelle said. "I'm not Cinderella, and my car doesn't turn into a pumpkin at midnight."

Amanda shook her head and then remembered that Michelle couldn't see it. "No. I can take a cab, and we'll see each other another time."

"Are you sure?"

"Yes. Remember you have that photo shoot at dawn on Monday morning, and I don't want you to have to work on three hours of sleep. Your job is as important as mine."

Michelle became very quiet for a moment and then said, "Thank you."

"What for?"

"A lot of my exes never saw it that way. They thought just pressing the shutter of a camera a few times wasn't much of a job."

Amanda snorted. "Just like pretending to be someone else on TV isn't much of a job."

"Guess so."

"I wish it were that way. Then I wouldn't have to hang up now to study my lines for tomorrow."

"That's all right," Michelle said. "I have to get going in a few minutes too."

"Oh, hot date?" Amanda kept her tone light but couldn't help feeling a bit insecure. They hadn't talked about where their relationship was going and whether they wanted to be exclusive.

"You could say that. I'm meeting a good-looking actress to watch an episode of *The Golden Girls* and possibly *Ellen*."

It took a few seconds for Amanda to understand. "You're meeting my grandmother?"

"Yes. I drove over to watch *Central Precinct* with her yesterday too. I hope that's okay?"

"Of course. Why wouldn't it be?"

"I don't know. I just don't want you to think that I'm trying to get into her good graces to earn brownie points with you."

Amanda hadn't thought that for even a second. She knew that Michelle was not that kind of person. "You think you need brownie points?"

"Can't hurt. But I'm spending time with your grandmother because I like her and because she's lonely without your grandfather, especially since you left for Vegas."

Tears stung Amanda's eyes. "I know. I'm trying to spend as much time as possible with her, but with this new role and…"

"And this new relationship," Michelle said when Amanda trailed off. "Listen, I want you to know that I'm not making any demands on your time. I know you have to focus on other things right now. With your job and your grandmother, you have enough on your plate."

An echo of something her first agent had once told her ricocheted through Amanda's mind. *If you want to make it in Hollywood, say good-bye to your private life. If you want to date, date someone in the business. With the crazy hours you'll work, plus press junkets, interviews, and after-parties, it'll never work with someone else.* More tears came, and she angrily dashed them away. Why was she so emotional today? Being away from home for a few days had never affected her this much before. "You're not breaking up with me, are you?" She tried to make it sound like a joke, but some of her insecurity leaked through.

"Hell, no."

The determination in Michelle's voice chased away the remainders of Amanda's tears. "With me on location or shooting all of the time, it's not gonna be easy."

"Are *you* trying to break up with me?"

"I'm trying to give you an out," Amanda said.

"I don't want one."

Silence filled the line for several seconds.

Amanda pressed the phone closer to her ear and whispered, "I don't want one either."

"Good." Michelle's voice, deep and husky, rumbled through the phone. "I have to get going, or I'll be late for my date with my second-favorite actress. Do you want me to call you later to practice some lines?"

"Why does that sound dirty?"

Michelle chuckled. "Must be because you have a dirty mind. My intentions are pure. Well, most of them. So, do we have a date later?"

"You mean a rehearsal." Amanda smiled at the old joke between them. "Our official date won't be before Valentine's Day, remember?"

"Right. So, *rehearsal* later?"

"I'm counting on it," Amanda said. She had come to love talking to Michelle right before she went to sleep. "Give my grandmother a hug from me."

"Will do. Until later."

For several minutes after they had hung up, Amanda lay on the bed, the phone pressed to her chest until a knock on the door and the call, "room service" startled her out of her thoughts and out of bed.

"If you move even one inch, I'm gonna shoot your stupid head off!" Amanda said, putting a snarl into her voice.

Paper rustled on the other end of the line. "Uh, *stupid* isn't in the script. At least not in the version you faxed me."

Amanda glanced down at her own copy of the script. Damn. Michelle was right. Amanda cleared her throat and tried again. "If you move even one fucking inch, I'm gonna shoot your head off!"

Instead of delivering her line, Michelle laughed. "I get the feeling you don't like the guy playing your suspect."

"Huh? Why?"

"*Fucking* isn't in the script either."

Amanda checked the script—which, of course, had no profanity at all—and groaned. "I like him just fine, but the script isn't as good as our other episodes." She grabbed the stack of paper and threw it toward the bottom of the bed.

"No? What we've read so far seems pretty interesting to me."

"The plot is, kind of, but the bad guy's motivation makes no sense at all." Amanda leaned against the headboard and kicked the script off the bed with her bare toes. "I mean he's a bookkeeper who normally couldn't even hurt a fly. But then, out of the blue, he kills a man he has never even met before. Slits his throat for no good reason."

"Oh, he had a very good reason," Michelle said. "Love."

The tone of her voice sent the by now familiar tingles up and down Amanda's body. She forced herself to focus on the conversation. "Love?" She snorted. "He and the casino owner's daughter don't even exchange more than two words during the whole episode. They barely know each other."

"All right. Maybe it's not love. Maybe it's lust. Who could blame the poor guy? You said the casino owner's daughter is played by Grace Durand, and that woman is hot!"

"Hot?" An emotion that felt very much like jealousy pierced Amanda with its ugly claws.

"Sizzling. Don't you think so?"

"I guess."

"You guess?" Michelle sounded incredulous. "She's been on every sexiest-woman-alive list known to mankind for several years in a row, and she just turned down a six-figure offer from *Playboy*."

"Is that how you spend your time while I'm in Vegas? Reading my grandmother's celebrity gossip rags?" Amanda asked, chuckling.

"No, I don't need to read the gossip rags to know that. It's common knowledge. Just like the fact that she's hot."

All right, Grace Durand was gorgeous, but Amanda still didn't like that open admiration in Michelle's voice when she talked about the world-famous actress. "Yeah, well, I guess it depends on what you find attractive in a woman."

A rustling noise sounded as if Michelle had thrown the script off her bed too. "Oh, now it's getting interesting. What do you find attractive in a woman?"

Amanda thought about it for a minute. What was it that she first noticed about the women she had dated? If anyone had asked her a few months ago, she would have described a woman like Grace Durand too—long, blonde hair and luscious curves. Michelle had neither of these features, yet lately, she had starred in a lot of Amanda's fantasies.

"Come on," Michelle said when Amanda remained silent. "Tell me. What is it that sparks your interest?"

"Your...I mean *her* hands," Amanda said. She closed her eyes and imagined Michelle's strong hands and her long fingers. Immediately, her mind suggested several things those hands could do to her. "Oh, yeah, definitely her hands. And her ass." And her legs, her arms, and the way she smelled. Truth be told, she liked everything about Michelle. She opened her eyes before she could lose herself in her daydreams. "Maybe love isn't such a bad motivation for our bad guy after all."

Michelle laughed. "I thought you'd see it my way. So, want to continue practicing lines?"

"No." Amanda had thoroughly lost interest in the script. "I want to know what turns you on."

Silence.

"Michelle? You still there?"

"Um, yeah. Still here. My mind just went south for a moment." Michelle coughed. "Okay, so what was the question? Oh, yeah, right. Well, the first thing that catches my interest in a woman are her eyes. I'm a sucker for big blue eyes."

Check.

"And blonde hair."

Check.

"A killer smile and a nice pair of C cups don't hurt either."

Amanda playfully peered down her pajama top. *Check, I think.* She cleared her throat. "Uh, you do know that you're describing me, don't you? Well, me and half of the actresses in Hollywood, of course."

"That's because you didn't let me finish my list," Michelle said.

"Okay. What else is on that list?"

"Not what—who," Michelle said. "You. You are on the list. I'd say that narrows it down."

Amanda smiled. "Charmer."

"No, I mean it. In the past, my list of must-have characteristics stopped at the C cups, but over the last few years, I've realized that I want what my parents and my grandparents had and what my brother has with his wife. And for that, I need a woman who is independent yet values

143

monogamy and family. A woman with an adventurous spirit, but with both feet firmly on the ground. Someone who knows what she wants and goes after it, but not in a ruthless way. A woman like you."

Amanda didn't know what to say. She had never wanted to hold anyone so much in her life. Silently, she cursed each and every one of the two hundred and twenty-four miles between them.

"Does that scare you?" Michelle asked quietly. "Me talking like this? Comparing us to all the happily-ever-after couples in my family?"

"No. I like a woman who knows what she wants and goes after it too."

Michelle was silent for a few moments; then she sighed, a sound full of longing. "God, I can't wait to see you. Are you sure you don't want me to pick you up from the airport?"

What Amanda wanted wrestled with what she thought she had to do—and finally lost. "Yes, I'm sure. You need your sleep to be fit for the photo shoot on Monday morning." And she needed to let the director and the rest of the cast and crew believe that she was straight. She pressed her lips together. *I bet a woman trapped in Hollywood's celluloid closet is not on your list.*

"Cut! No, no, no. Not like that, Amanda." Walt stepped out from behind his monitor and walked over to Amanda, waving his hands at the rest of the cast as if to shoo them away. "Everybody, take five."

Amanda ducked her head at the groans of her colleagues. This was the fourth take already, but she just couldn't get the emotions right. She tried to calm down and focus, but that wasn't easy in her noisy surroundings. Slot machines jangled in the background, coins rattled into metal bins, and dealers chanted out numbers.

The part of the casino that they used as a set hummed like a beehive as production assistants herded two dozen extras back into their initial positions around the poker table and the slot machines. The crew readjusted the camera position and angled the lights.

A makeup artist, a hairstylist, and someone from wardrobe descended on Amanda and fussed over her hair, makeup, and clothes.

Ignoring them, Walt stopped in front of Amanda.

"Sorry, Walt," Amanda said. "For some reason, this is a tough one for me."

"Look around. What do you see?"

"A casino?"

Walt shook his head. "It's not just a casino for Linda Halliday. She's facing her biggest weakness in this scene. Something that could ruin her career, her whole life, yet she can't help wanting it."

Amanda knew that, of course, but it was still hard for her to get into her character's head and feel what Linda Halliday was feeling.

"Haven't you ever been addicted to something?" Walt asked. "Smoked some grass in high school or threw back too many beers?"

She had spent most of her high school years trying to keep her grades up while starring in her drama club's productions and coming to terms with the fact that she was gay, but she couldn't say that to Walt, so she just shook her head. She looked around, ignoring the crew, the bright lights, and the cameras, and tried to see the casino through Detective Halliday's eyes, tried to imagine craving something so badly that it was almost like an ache and you were ready to risk something important, just to satisfy that craving.

Had she ever felt something like that?

Her first spontaneous answer was a vehement no, but then a thought occurred to her.

Living in a shoebox-sized dive of an apartment for three years so she had enough money for an acting and voice coach... Going to an audition running a high fever, just for the chance of getting a bit role... Wasn't that a little on the obsessive side?

Another realization hit her.

What about Michelle? Staying up until three in the morning to talk to her on the phone, even though she knew she'd regret it in the morning... Being tempted to pay for an earlier flight home out of her own pocket, just so she could see Michelle on Sunday night... Was that what an addiction felt like?

No, a voice in her head said, sounding like that of her grandmother, *that's how it feels to be in love.*

Stunned, she stared at Walt. She couldn't be in love so soon, could she? She and Michelle had known each other for less than two months. They hadn't even gone on an official date yet. In her past relationships, it had taken her months to feel comfortable with calling it love. But to her heart, none of that seemed to matter.

"You okay?" Walt asked.

Amanda blinked. "Oh, yes. Yes. I'm fine. Just fine. I think I have a good angle now."

He patted her shoulder. "Good. Then let's try this scene again." He waved to the rest of the cast and ducked back behind his monitor as the camera dolly rolled back to its initial position.

"Quiet on set," someone hollered.

Amanda took her mark and tried to get deeply into her character, letting herself feel that strange mix of emotions that came with hearing Michelle's voice. It was soothing and familiar, almost like coming home, yet at the same time it was new and exciting and made her blood sing.

As if from far away, she heard the assistant director call, "Roll sound."

"Speed," one of the sound technicians answered.

"Roll camera."

"Rolling."

"Marker," the assistant director called.

The clapperboard cracked.

When Walt called, "action" and the camera moved in for the close-up, Amanda slowly unclenched her fingers and looked down at the dice in her palm. She looked at them as if they were something she had wanted all of her life but hadn't found so far. Now it was within reach, but it came with a price, just like this long-awaited role kept her from seeing Michelle again.

She stared at the dice, not knowing for how long; then she closed her fingers around them and lifted her hand as if wanting to throw them onto the green felt. At the last moment, she let them drop to the floor instead, turned, and walked away, shouldering through the crowd at the craps table.

"Cut," Walt called and rushed over to her.

The extras jumped out of the way.

Amanda swallowed. Had she ruined another take?

Walt grabbed her shoulder and shook her gently. "Fantastic! Whatever you were thinking of worked like a charm. You played it perfectly. Let's break for lunch, people!"

As he walked away, Amanda let a long breath escape.

Nick sauntered over. "That was great. This episode might earn you an Emmy."

That finally pulled Amanda out of her stupor. She gazed up at him. "You really think so?"

"Why not? The emotions on your face…wow. You really made me believe you were struggling with a gambling addiction."

"Uh, thanks."

"So, this is our last full day in Vegas. If we manage to wrap early, are you up for a little sightseeing tonight?" He gave her a hopeful glance.

Amanda groaned inwardly. "I thought you already did your sightseeing yesterday?"

"Yeah, but some things are worth seeing twice, especially in the right company."

She shook her head. "No, thanks."

"You're not much for sightseeing, are you? If you'd prefer, we could just grab a bite to eat or—"

"No, it's not that. Listen…" Amanda hesitated. Whenever one of her male colleagues had tried to ask her out in the past, she had just told him she was gay. But then she hadn't had a career to speak of, so she hadn't needed to worry about being typecast in "gay" roles from now on. Hollywood had changed along with society; coming out was no longer a career ender, but it could narrow her opportunities.

"Oh, I see," Nick said. "You're already seeing someone."

"Yes. It's still pretty fresh, but I think it has the potential to turn into something very special," Amanda said, not having to rely on her acting skills.

Nick's face fell. "Oh." Slowly, the grin reappeared. "Well, the offer still stands. After all, what happens on location stays on location, right?"

"Tempting," she said, hiding a sarcastic smirk, "but I'm the old-fashioned, loyal type, so thanks, but no thanks."

Nick shrugged. "Your loss," he said and walked away.

Hmph. Actors. Why would anyone want to date a Hollywood star with an ego the size of California? Of course, she was glad that Michelle had changed her mind about that. Still shaking her head, she joined Lorena at the catering table they had set up in their part of the casino. After talking to Michelle until three in the morning, she had overslept and hadn't had time for breakfast. Now her stomach was growling. She reached for a bagel and took a big bite.

Lorena turned, a fruit cup in her hands. She watched as Amanda devoured her bagel. "I don't know how you can eat like this and stay so slim." Sighing, she nibbled on a piece of pineapple.

With her mouth full, Amanda just shrugged. She would rather eat whatever she wanted and then spend some time in the gym than having to watch every bite she ate.

"And you get to have all the fun on set too. All I do all day is cut open bodies and spout medical terminology, while you get to play in the casino. What's up with that, huh?" Lorena elbowed one of the show's writers, who nearly spilled his coffee.

He put down the Styrofoam cup and held up his hands. "What do you expect? This is a crime show, and you're playing the medical examiner."

"Yeah, but how about a little change of pace? Maybe you could write a romance into the script or something."

Amanda shook her head. "Oh, please, don't encourage him, or they'll end up having Halliday make googly eyes at her partner." She liked her character the way the writers had created her—flawed, but strong and independent.

"Naw." Lorena grimaced. "No chemistry between the two of you. Guess tall, dark, and handsome isn't your type."

Amanda hid a grin. "Oh, I like tall, dark, and handsome just fine."

Lorena regarded her with a knowing smile. "I see. You have your own tall, dark, and handsome someone waiting for you at home."

Not wanting to get herself into a situation where she had to lie about Michelle's gender, Amanda just nodded. "How about you? Someone waiting for you at home?"

Lorena put down her fruit cup and pulled an engagement ring that she was wearing on a chain out from under her shirt. "Boring Dr. Castellano is single, so I can't wear it while we're shooting."

"Oh, wow. You're engaged? I didn't know."

"Yeah, well, with all the media attention the show has been getting since the Emmys, I'm trying to keep the job and my private life separate."

Amanda would have to do that too, even more so than Lorena. She bit her lip. "Are you happy? I mean... Relationships aren't easy under the best of circumstances, but with location shoots and our crazy schedules... How do you make it work?"

"Rafe is a teacher, so he can travel with me when I shoot on location during the summer. But I'm not gonna lie to you. It's not easy during the rest of the year. We manage with lots of phone calls." Lorena forced a smile and wiggled her eyebrows. "And lots of cold showers."

"Ooh, so that's why you're asking for a little on-screen romance," the writer said. "Sexual frustration."

Lorena answered with a snarky remark, but Amanda didn't listen to their banter. She could see a lot of cold showers in her future too.

CHAPTER 8

WHEN THEY LANDED AT LAX and got off the plane, Amanda nearly fell to her knees and kissed the ground. Filming in Vegas had been great, but she'd never been so glad to be back home.

As they left the luggage area, Nick was instantly surrounded by a dozen female fans asking for autographs and Lorena was whirled around and kissed senseless by a hunk of a man, whom she introduced as her fiancé.

Amanda stood alone with her suitcase and missed Michelle so fiercely that it hurt. *You told her not to come, remember?* Sighing, she followed her colleagues out of the glass sliding doors—and stumbled to a stop.

In the short-term parking area, Michelle leaned against her SUV and beamed at her.

Amanda blinked, for a moment not sure if she was real or just a figment of her imagination. But then Michelle lifted her hand and waved. Amanda wanted to dash over and greet her the way Lorena had greeted her fiancé, but with her colleagues right there, she didn't dare.

Michelle had taken a step in Amanda's direction but then hesitated when Amanda didn't move toward her.

"Hey, Amanda," Lorena called and looked over her shoulder at her. "You coming? Rafe can drive you home."

"Uh, no, that won't be necessary. Someone's here to pick me up." She gestured in Michelle's direction.

Lorena glanced toward the SUV and its driver. "Ah, the hot boyfriend that had you glued to the phone whenever we weren't shooting."

The longer Amanda knew Michelle, the less she understood how anyone could mistake her for a man. Those kissable lips were much too soft to be a man's. "Uh, yeah, something like that."

Lorena might have answered, but Amanda was no longer listening. Drawn in by those gentle brown eyes, she crossed the parking area. With the suitcase between them, she stopped and just looked at her from a yard away. Back in Vegas, she had dreamed about what she'd do when she saw Michelle again, but her fantasies hadn't included her colleagues watching or her sudden shyness.

"Hi," Michelle said softly. "You okay?"

Amanda nodded and, colleagues be damned, let herself sink into Michelle's arms, almost stumbling over her suitcase in the process.

Michelle pushed the suitcase out of the way and immediately pulled her close. "Are you really okay?" she whispered into Amanda's hair.

Burrowing deeper into Michelle's leather jacket and breathing in her scent, Amanda nodded again. "Just tired. We were shooting right up until we had to leave for the airport, and then some kid kicked the back of my seat all the way from Vegas to LA." She hesitated but then decided to be honest. "And, well..." She glanced over her shoulder at her colleagues, who were loading their suitcases into the trunk and the backseat of Rafe's car. "My co-stars don't know I'm gay."

"Oh." Michelle let go and stepped back. "Was that why you didn't want me to pick you up?"

At the hurt in her voice, Amanda followed her with two quick steps and wrapped her arms around her again, consequences be damned. "No. Mainly, I really wanted you to stay home because I want you well rested for your photo shoot tomorrow. It's just... I don't know what this could mean for my career. Hollywood people can't keep a secret to save their lives, so if I come out to my colleagues, it'll be all over LA in a matter of hours."

"Some can," Michelle said. "Your grandmother didn't tell you I'd come to pick you up, did she?"

"She knew? No, she never said a word, that sneaky old woman. How is she?"

"Same as me," Michelle said, gazing into her eyes. "Missing you."

"I missed you too. I'm glad you didn't listen and came to pick me up." Amanda lifted up on her tiptoes and, clutching Michelle's muscular back beneath the open leather jacket, pressed their lips together. The kiss instantly deepened.

One of Michelle's hands slid beneath her blouse and touched the bare skin of her back, setting every inch of her on fire.

With a moan, Amanda pressed closer and slipped one leg between Michelle's thighs.

The sound of Michelle's keys hitting the ground startled them apart. Only then did Amanda notice that Rafe's car had pulled away without her noticing. Breathing heavily, she leaned her head against Michelle's chest.

Michelle trailed her fingers over Amanda's neck, sending goose bumps up and down her spine.

"Well," Michelle said and then stopped to clear her throat. "Guess you're out now."

Amanda shook her head, enjoying the sliding of the smooth leather against her cheek. "Lorena thinks you're a man, and I didn't correct her." She looked up to study Michelle's flushed face. "Does that bother you?"

"I'd lie if I said it didn't, but I know it's not easy to be out as an actress in Hollywood. I'll support you and your choices, no matter what."

That show of support made Amanda feel even more guilty. "But you're out and proud, right?"

Michelle nodded. "I've been out to everyone and their dog since I watched *Spur of the Moment* at the age of five and declared to my whole family that I'd marry Josephine Mabry when I grew up."

Amanda laughed, totally charmed. She'd have to tell this story to her grandmother. Even at eighty-two, no actress would ever be immune to being flattered like that. "What did your family say?"

"Nothing. They just stared at me in shocked silence. Then my grandfather cleared his throat and said, 'Well, she's a fine-looking lady, but...don't you think she might be a tad too old for you?'"

"Your grandfather really sounds great." Actually, he sounded a lot like Michelle.

"He was. I think back to that positive first experience whenever I come out to someone. Not that I have much of a choice, anyway. People take one look at me and just assume that I'm a lesbian. It's a stereotype, but in my case, it's true."

Amanda sighed. Having a choice didn't make life any easier. She rubbed her eyes, which were burning from lack of sleep and the stuffy air on the plane.

"Come on." Michelle massaged the back of Amanda's neck for a moment before sliding her hand lower, to the small of her back, and guiding her toward the SUV. "Let's get you home and into bed."

The words sent a tingle through Amanda's tired body, even though she knew Michelle hadn't meant it the way it had sounded. *Soon,* she promised herself. *Very soon.*

"We really have to stop meeting like this," Michelle said as they once again stood in front of Amanda's apartment building, both of them hesitating to say good-bye, even though Amanda was yawning every few seconds.

Michelle shifted her hold on the suitcase that she had insisted on carrying, drawing Amanda's attention once again to her strong hands.

On the way from the airport, she had turned on the light inside of the SUV and gripped the steering wheel in a way that made the tendons and muscles in her hands stand out.

"Stop it." Amanda reached out and lightly slapped her ass. "I know what you're doing."

"Me?" Michelle pressed one of her hands to her chest.

"Yeah, you. See, you're doing it again. You're torturing me, drawing attention to your hands at every opportunity, just because I told you I like them."

Michelle shook her head. "Oh, no, that's not torture; believe me. Torture is wanting to come up with you so much it hurts, but knowing it's not a good idea."

Amanda toyed with the top button of her blouse as she remembered the last time Michelle had accompanied her up to her apartment. That elevator ride had been replayed in her mind on many lonely nights since then.

"And torture is the way you're playing with your button, drawing attention to your nice pair of C cups."

"Oops." Amanda realized what she was doing and let go of the button. "I'm sorry. The spirit is more than willing, but the flesh is weak."

"I know. You look like you're about to fall over and not because I swept you off your feet."

"Yeah. I'm really beat." Calling up emotions for the camera all day, while operating on just a few hours of sleep, had been exhausting.

"Let me carry that suitcase up for you."

"So you can torture me some more by flexing your ass too?" Amanda shook her head. "No, thanks."

As if by mutual agreement, they kept their good-night kiss short and sweet. When Michelle pulled her into her arms for a hug, Amanda buried her face against Michelle's neck, breathing her in and wishing she could fall asleep surrounded by that scent. If they stood there for much longer, she probably would. "Heavenly," she mumbled.

Michelle pulled back a few inches to look at her. "Did you just say 'heavenly'?" A smirk spread over her face.

"Can I help it when the way you smell is torture too?" Amanda buried her now hot face against Michelle's neck for a few moments longer and then pressed a kiss to her skin before letting go. "Call me when you get home so that I know you made it safely."

"No. You'll be sound asleep by the time I make it home, and I don't want to wake you."

"Call me," Amanda said more firmly.

Michelle sighed. "I just had to say that I want a woman who knows what she wants."

Amanda smiled and suppressed another yawn. "Seems you got your wish."

"Yeah, I did." Michelle kissed her again and then stepped back before the kiss could heat up and walked away.

Amanda watched her until she reached the SUV, got in, and drove off. When her taillights disappeared in the distance, she made her way, bleary-eyed, to the elevator. She was asleep before her head hit the pillow and never even woke when Michelle called her half an hour later.

CHAPTER 9

"WHEN WILL YOU BE HOME tomorrow night?" Michelle asked when Amanda called her right before bedtime, as had become their habit. "I thought I could invite you to a restaurant of your choice for a da...uh...rehearsal."

Amanda sighed. "I'd love to *rehearse* with you, but we're doing night shoots tomorrow. We could do something tomorrow morning, though. I don't have to be on set before noon, so if you have the time..."

Michelle groaned. "Sorry. I have an offer from a publishing house to put together a book with my photos of elderly people, and they want to talk about the details tomorrow morning."

"Oh, wow, that's wonderful! Congratulations!" Amanda was so proud that she felt as if she would burst any moment.

"Yeah, but I'm not celebrating until I sign the contract. Or better yet until I hold the book in my hands."

"Hey, why so gloomy? Where's your positive attitude?"

Michelle sighed. "It really is a great opportunity. Both of our careers are going great, but sometimes I can't help thinking that we'll never get to spend any time together. Is it just my imagination, or are you working even more than usual?"

"Yeah. We're shooting a storyline that arcs over several episodes in which Detective Halliday is kidnapped, so I have more airtime than usual." Which was good for her career, but it also sucked, because it cut short any time she might have with Michelle or her grandmother.

Michelle was silent for a while.

"You okay?"

"Yeah. I just spaced out at the word *kidnapping*. Maybe that's the way to go if I want to spend some uninterrupted time with you."

"I'm sorry." Her shooting schedule had been a recipe for burnout since they had returned to LA last week, and she didn't see it changing anytime soon.

"No. No need to apologize. This is your job, and you're damn good at it. Your grandmother and I watched that episode where they have you chase that suspect through the forest. Pretty intense."

Amanda groaned. "That scene took about a thousand takes until we got it right. Walt prefers not to use stunt doubles for all but the most dangerous scenes, so he had me jump across that river. Well, okay, it was more like a creek, but I nearly broke my leg anyway."

"Yeah, that looked pretty dangerous. Your grandmother was a bit worried."

"And you?" Amanda asked, only half teasing. "Were you worried too?"

"Not worried, mostly, but when you tackled the suspect..." She cleared her throat. "Let's just say I would have given an arm, a leg, and my favorite camera to have a tumble in the forest with you."

Her voice got hoarser with every word, and in response, a ball of heat formed low in Amanda's belly. "You do know that I have to go to bed now? To my cold, lonely bed. To sleep. And you're not exactly making me sleepy."

Michelle laughed.

God, I love that sound.

"So you're ready for bed, hmm?" Michelle drawled. "What are you wearing?"

"Oh, no, no, no. Don't do that to me."

"What am I doing to you?" Michelle asked in a tone that was pure seduction.

Amanda slid her fingertips beneath the edge of her panties. Heat radiated off her skin. She squeezed her eyes shut and stopped the downward motion of her hand. "I could tell you," she said in much the same tone of voice. "But I'd rather show you."

Michelle's breath audibly hitched. "I could be there in half an hour, give or take a few traffic infractions."

Were they still just teasing? Amanda wasn't sure. Her body screamed at her to say yes, but one last bit of reason held her back. "It's the most tempting offer I've gotten since that call from *Central Precinct*, but I want more than just a quickie, with one of us sneaking out in the middle of the night because of an early-morning call time or a photo shoot."

What a departure from her usual dating script. Normally, she just went with the flow, without taking care to build a solid basis for her relationships first. Maybe that was part of the reason why they never lasted for very long.

"I want that too," Michelle said, now all hints of teasing gone from her voice. She inhaled and exhaled noisily. "Be careful on that night shoot tomorrow. No dangerous stunts and no tumbles in the forest with Lorena Gonzales."

Amanda laughed. "Don't worry. Lorena is engaged to that hunk who carried her suitcase, and I'm pretty stuck on someone too."

"Pretty stuck, hmm?" From the sound of her voice, Michelle was grinning from ear to ear. "Well, that someone is pretty stuck on you too."

"Does that mean no making out with models during photo shoots?"

"No, sadly, that's not part of my job perks. Unless... I could take some photos of you on your next day off. I know your grandmother's birthday is coming up, and I'm sure she'd love to have a new photo of you."

For someone who made her living in front of the camera, Amanda hated being photographed, but maybe it would be different with Michelle behind the camera. "All right. It's a date."

"A date?"

Laughing, Amanda rolled her eyes. "Date. Rehearsal. Call it whatever you want."

"It's a date, then. Definitely a date. Just call me whenever you have the time. Oh, and Amanda? Dress sexy."

"Sexy?"

"I was thinking a lacy bra and—"

Amanda shook her head. "I don't think my grandmother would appreciate that for her birthday photo."

"Maybe your grandmother won't, but I sure will."

"Letch."

"Yes," Michelle said, "but I'm *your* letch."

They were both silent for several seconds, quietly acknowledging how their relationship had changed. Finally, Amanda cleared her throat and said, "Yes, you are. Goodnight."

"Goodnight. Sweet dreams."

Amanda's hair was plastered to her forehead, and she had to fight the urge to wipe the sweat off her face, knowing it would ruin her artfully applied special-effects makeup, including the fake bruises around her eyes, the bleeding cut between her eyebrows, and the abrasions on her left cheek.

Every muscle hurt from lying on the hard wood floor, tied up like a parcel, and the rope binding her hands cut into her skin. Grumpily, she thought that they soon wouldn't need any stage tricks to make her wrists look as if the ropes had chaffed at them for hours.

"Ready?" Walt asked.

Amanda nodded. *Ready to get out of here.*

Because the tapes would pick up the sound, they had to shut off air conditioning while they were shooting, and the camera and lights in front of Amanda gave out heat like flamethrowers from an action movie.

Sound and camera started rolling. The slate operator closed the clapper sticks with a loud crack and hurried away, into a corner of their set that was an imitation of a cabin in the woods.

"Action," the assistant director called.

Amanda started writhing against the ropes binding her arms and legs. She didn't have to act to turn her face into a mask of pain and exhaustion.

From his place behind the monitor that showed him the camera feed, Walt gave her a sign when it was time to free one of her hands.

Amanda tried, but the stubborn rope wasn't cooperating.

"Cut." Walt walked over. "What's going on? Why aren't you slipping free of the rope?"

"It's too tight. I can't get out." Amanda turned so he could see her bound wrists.

"Damn. You're bleeding. What idiot made it so tight?" Cursing, he turned and waved at the nearest PA. "Cathy, get me a doctor in here and—"

"No," Amanda said. "I'm fine. Let's just get this scene filmed before we break for lunch."

"If you're sure…"

"I am sure." If they waited for a doctor to check out the superficial cuts on her wrists, they'd never wrap up shooting in time for her to call Michelle before she went to bed.

"All right."

While Amanda waited for the PA to loosen the rope and for the camera to roll back into the initial position, she carefully channeled her impatience into her role. She slipped back into the body and mind of Detective Linda Halliday, determined to make it out of the cabin and the clutches of her kidnapper alive.

This time, one of her hands came free at the correct moment. Without freeing her other hand, she struggled with the rope around her feet until that fell away too. She raced to the door, stumbling for a moment, as the script demanded, because circulation had been cut off for too long.

Just as she fumbled with the bolt, the door swung open, pushing her back, and a gorilla of a man pounced on her.

They landed on the rough-hewn wood floor, with him on top.

Uff. Some very real bruises would no doubt cover her back and her ribs by tonight. She drove her knee between his legs, remembering at the last moment to pull her punch.

He grunted, and she dove for his weapon.

"Cut!" Walt yelled.

Amanda flopped to the wood floor. What was it now? From her position on the floor, she peered up at Walt.

"That looked way too easy."

Easy? Amanda gritted her teeth.

"We want our audience to suffer along with Detective Halliday. They can't do that if they don't believe she's in mortal danger." Walt turned to the actor playing the psychopath kidnapper. "When she goes for your weapon, you could try choking her. Do either of you want a stunt double for that?"

Amanda immediately shook her head. Maybe it was dumb, but she was proud of doing most of the action scenes herself, even if Michelle would no doubt tease her about her butchness rubbing off on her.

"All right. Then let's go again." Walt waved at the PA with the rope.

Amanda held still while Cathy rebound her hands. Her mind flashed back to Michelle's joke about her bringing back handcuffs from the set, and she wondered what Michelle would think about this scene.

"You're an awfully good sport about this," Cathy said. "I've never known an actor who was still grinning after four takes of this hell."

Only then did Amanda realize that she was smiling. "They didn't have my motivation."

The PA lifted one eyebrow. "Which is?"

Amanda just smiled and, channeling her detective character, said, "I'm pleading the fifth."

A knock on her trailer door startled Amanda awake. Groaning, she realized that she had fallen asleep when she had lain down on the couch in her trailer to study her lines for the next scene. Jesus, had she missed her call time? She struggled into an upright position and glanced at her watch.

No, it was still half an hour before she had to be back on set.

When the knock came again, she got up from the couch. Intimately familiar with the layout of the trailer by now, she found her way to the door in the darkness and opened it.

For a second, she thought she was still dreaming.

Michelle stood on the top step, backlit by the lights from the parking lot where the trailers were parked.

Amanda stared at her, afraid to move or even blink, as if this vision would disappear if she did.

"Hi," Michelle said softly. She lifted a small cooler. "I hope you don't mind me visiting you at work. I thought I'd bring you something to eat."

"Mind?" Amanda still couldn't stop staring. "God, no. You coming here is the best thing that happened to me all day, and not just because I'm starving. But..." She frowned. "How did you make it past the security guys at the studio gate?" Since the popularity of the show had increased, security was much stricter.

A grin crossed Michelle's face. "I have my ways."

"You didn't climb the fence, did you?"

"No. I still have my press pass, and I told them *People* magazine sent me to do an interview with you. So, can I come in since I came bearing gifts?"

"Of course. Come in and tell me all about that meeting with the publisher."

"Not much to tell. Could be a year until the book is published, but so far, it looks like it'll go through."

"Great. Congratulations again." Amanda threw her arms around her and buried her face against Michelle's shoulder. Instantly, the tension drained from her body, and she relaxed for the first time all day.

"Hey." Michelle's free hand came up, and she cradled the back of Amanda's head in one palm. "You all right?"

Amanda nodded, her face still pressed against the leather jacket. "Yes. I just needed a hug."

"Bad day?" Michelle rubbed her back.

"Long day," Amanda said. "And it's not over yet. I get to do another tumble-in-the-forest scene in an hour, but this time, I'm the one being chased."

Michelle slid her fingers through Amanda's hair and gently massaged her scalp, making her groan in delight. "Are you wishing back the good old days of shooting commercials with bitchy camels and misbehaving cats?"

Amanda laughed and finally pulled back. "No. It's tough, but I love it. This is the role that I've been trying to get for the past—"

"Four years, four months, and about twenty-four days," Michelle said.

The numbers sounded about right. "You remember?"

"Of course. I remember everything you ever said to me, including that promise to come over in nothing but sexy underwear and let me ravish...um, I mean...photograph you."

"I don't remember it quite that way." Amanda pulled Michelle fully into the trailer, closed the door behind her, and turned on the light.

"Must be all this overtime affecting your memory. You—" The teasing reply died on Michelle's lips. Her eyes widened as she got her first good look at Amanda's face. She dropped the cooler and gently touched Amanda's cheek. "Oh my God, what happened?"

It took Amanda a moment to figure out what she meant. "Oh, that. Don't worry; it's not real. Just some makeup magic."

Michelle blew out a breath. "Wow. It looks so real." She tilted her head and studied the cuts and bruises on Amanda's face from all angles and then touched the rope burns at her wrist.

Amanda flinched. "Ouch. That one is real."

Gently, Michelle lifted one of Amanda's hands and frowned at the abrasion as if it were a mortal wound. "How did that happen?"

"Oh, just a little bondage play with Lorena between takes."

Michelle looked up from Amanda's wrist. Her eyes held a mix of concern and humor before they darkened. "No more playtime for Lorena. You're mine."

"Oh, yeah?"

"Yeah." Michelle lifted Amanda's hand and gently touched her lips to the injured wrist, then tugged her forward until their bodies collided and kissed her. In contrast with the gentle kiss to her wrist, this one was passionate and possessive.

Heat flared through Amanda. She grabbed the lapels of the leather jacket, pulled Michelle even closer, and took possession of the kiss, nipping Michelle's bottom lip and sliding her tongue into her mouth.

They tumbled onto the couch, with Amanda on top.

Groaning, Michelle pulled her into the V of her legs and tried to roll them around, but Amanda refused to give up her position.

With her hands pressed to Michelle's shoulders to hold her down, she looked down at her. "Maybe you are mine."

"Oh, yeah?"

"Yeah." Amanda let her lips wander down the side of her neck, kissing and nipping at every inch of skin, hungry for its taste and smell.

A hurried rap on the trailer door stopped her cold.

Cursing, she rolled off Michelle, marched over to the door, and threw it open. "What?"

A young PA stood frozen on the top step of her trailer, holding up his clipboard like a shield. "Uh, makeup wants you to come over. They need to touch up your makeup and the fake wounds before shooting continues."

Amanda fought the urge to glance over her shoulder at Michelle. "Do I have time for a quick bite first?"

"Guess so."

"All right. I'll be there in five." Not waiting for a reply, she closed the door and turned.

Michelle had gotten up from the couch and was rummaging through the cooler she had brought. Her well-shaped backside instantly caught Amanda's attention. "What do you want?" Michelle asked without turning around. "I've got some fruit and—"

Amanda knew what she wanted, and it had nothing to do with the contents of the cooler. "How about a kiss to go?"

Michelle straightened and turned. Her eyes were smoldering. "God, you make me so—"

Amanda stepped closer and captured her mouth with hers. She had only five minutes to kiss her senseless, after all, so she had to make good use of that time.

CHAPTER 10

"WE'D BETTER HANG UP NOW." Amanda clutched the phone as if that would help close the physical distance separating her from Michelle. "I have a seven o'clock call for publicity photos at the studio tomorrow morning, so I need to get a good night's sleep."

"You're not nervous, are you?" Michelle asked.

At first, Amanda wanted to deny it. After all, what kind of actress became nervous at the thought of having her picture taken? But then she reminded herself that she was talking to Michelle and didn't have to put up a strong front. "A little."

"But you're in front of the camera all day long."

"Not that kind of camera. The only time I was in front of that kind of camera was when I got my actor headshots done. And my colleagues won't even be there for support. Since I joined the show mid-season, I'm the only one without publicity shots."

"Don't worry," Michelle said. "You'll do just fine. I bet the camera loves you."

What about the photographer? Amanda wanted to ask but didn't dare. Every time Michelle looked at her, she saw more than desire in her eyes, but it wasn't fair to force her to say the words before she was ready.

"What's that sigh for?"

Amanda hadn't realized she'd been sighing. "Uh, nothing. Just wishing it was you taking the photos instead of some guy the studio hired."

"Well, you and I still have a date...uh, a rehearsal with a Nikon and a pair of lacy underwear."

The thought of Michelle seeing her in next to nothing sent shivers down her body. "Thanks. I'll never go to sleep now."

"But at least you're no longer thinking about tomorrow."

Amanda smiled. "If that was your intention, you definitely succeeded." She glanced at her alarm clock. Why was it that every time she talked to Michelle, time just seemed to rush by? "We really should hang up now."

"I know. Good night. And don't worry about tomorrow. You'll be in good hands."

"Good night. And thanks for the pep talk." Only when she had ended the call and settled down in bed did she start to wonder what Michelle had meant. *In good hands?* That thought made her start thinking about how Michelle's hands might look gripping a camera...and doing other, more exciting things. Groaning, she punched her pillow into submission and willed herself to go to sleep. She had to look her best tomorrow.

When Amanda finished in the makeup trailer and headed over to the set, where the publicity photos would be taken, several people were setting up light stands and white umbrellas.

Amanda swallowed her nervousness, put on her actor face, and headed over to where one of the show's producers was standing.

"Ah, Amanda." The producer smiled when he saw her. "Looks like they're almost ready for you." He gestured to someone who was bent over some kind of camera equipment.

Well, at least their photographer had a nice ass.

After making one final adjustment to the camera, the photographer straightened and turned.

Amanda froze. *What the...?*

"This is Michelle Osinski, your photographer for today. Ms. Osinski, this is Amanda Clark, who plays Detective Halliday." The producer looked at Michelle. "Do you have everything you need?"

Her gaze on Amanda, Michelle nodded.

"Great." The producer gave Amanda an encouraging pat on the shoulder. "Then I'll leave you in Ms. Osinski's capable hands." He walked away, leaving Amanda to stare at Michelle.

"What are you doing here?"

"Taking photos of a beautiful woman." Michelle's gaze slid over Amanda's detective clothes—black jeans, a red blouse, and the chocolate-colored leather jacket Amanda had come to love. "Not the kind of photos I'd prefer, but still..."

Amanda was still gaping at her. "How did you get this job?"

"An old college buddy of mine was supposed to do the shoot, but when he told me about it, I convinced him to contract a sudden case of malaria or laryngitis or something, offered my services to your producer—and here I am." Michelle swept her hand at herself and grinned. "I wanted it to be a surprise, so I didn't say anything. Hope you don't mind."

"Don't mind?" Amanda repeated. "This is the best surprise since…since you came over in the middle of the night to make me breakfast." She wanted to cross the last yard between them and wrap her arms around her, but a young man walked over to them.

"We're all set up, boss."

Michelle nodded without looking away from Amanda. "Are you ready to get started?"

Time to be a professional. "Yes. How do you want me?"

Something flickered in Michelle's eyes; then she, too, put on her professional façade. "Why don't we start with you leaning against your desk?"

They walked over to the part of the set that held the detectives' desks, loaded down with fake paperwork, and Amanda leaned against hers. "Like this?"

"Yeah. Move your legs a little farther apart. We want you to look casual, but confident." Michelle swept her arm in a gesture that included the entire fictional police station. "This is your territory, so don't be afraid to own it."

Amanda widened her stance.

"Exactly. See? I told you you'd be good at this. Don't think about the camera. Just you and me here."

Even with the assistants and crew bustling around behind them, that was easy to imagine.

"Now put your left hand on your belt, right next to the badge, and the right hand more back, not quite touching the gun."

Amanda did it.

Michelle turned on her camera and lifted it to her face, looking at Amanda through the viewfinder. "Great. Hold that pose." She strode away from Amanda, checked the lighting and the setup one final time, and then turned back around. She looked down at her camera, adjusting some setting with a quick flick of her finger, before holding the viewfinder up to eye level again.

The moment Michelle snapped the first picture, a transformation seemed to take place. Gone was Amanda's easygoing girlfriend. In her place stood a woman who exuded confidence. Energy radiated off her as she moved left and right to get better angles, the camera held with a steady underhand grip while the long fingers of her right hand pressed the shutter release button and adjusted the settings.

Amanda forgot her nervousness as she watched Michelle in action, watched the confident way she handled the camera, which looked as if it were an extension of her hands. *God, she's beautiful. She should have been in front of the camera, not behind it. And those hands...*

"God, yes, that's good. Keep this intense expression. Don't smile." Michelle crouched and took a few shots at an upward angle, rotating the zoom ring with a smooth motion of her left hand.

The soft clicking of the camera shutter, the whine of the flash as it recharged, and Michelle's footsteps echoed through the set. Nothing else seemed to exist, just Amanda, Michelle, and the camera. Amanda lost all sense of time.

Finally, Michelle lowered the camera a little, and their gazes met without the lens between them.

Her features knit in concentration, Michelle studied her, examining her so closely that Amanda felt for one strange moment as if Michelle was the only person who had ever looked at her—looked at her and really saw her.

After a few more moments, Michelle looked away, breaking the spell, and waved her assistant over. "I need more light on her right side. Can you set up a reflector?"

"You got it, boss." He hurried away to do her bidding.

The makeup artist used the opportunity to give Amanda's nose a dab of powder.

Michelle walked over with a bottle of water, the camera looped around her neck. "Here."

Gratefully, Amanda accepted the bottle, only now realizing how parched she was. She'd had no idea how physically and mentally demanding a photo shoot could be. She gulped down half of the bottle's contents and then wiped a drop of water off her bottom lip.

The snap of the camera made her look up. She tilted her head in a silent question.

"For my private collection," Michelle said with an almost shy grin. "All right. Back to work. Let's try a different pose."

Amanda handed the bottle to one of the assistants.

"Angle your body away from me, but keep facing forward. Look right at me. And tip your chin up. Perfect!" More snaps of the camera. "Roll your left shoulder back just a little bit."

When Amanda followed instructions, the ends of her leather jacket fell forward, covering the service weapon on her belt.

Michelle stopped snapping away and walked toward her. She reached out and pulled the leather jacket back to reveal the holster again. Then she straightened the collar of Amanda's blouse and pushed a wayward strand of hair behind her ear. Her fingers grazed the side of Amanda's face.

It was an innocent touch, an artist shaping her creation, but Amanda felt it to the core of her being. She held her breath and gazed into Michelle's eyes from just inches away.

"There. That's better." Michelle quickly turned and put some distance between them. She lifted the camera to her face as if hiding behind it.

So Amanda wasn't the only one being affected by the energy of the photo shoot.

"Don't smile," Michelle called.

Amanda wiped the grin off her face but continued to smile inwardly.

"Thanks. Just a few more seconds and we're done." After several more rapid-fire clicks, Michelle lowered the camera and regarded her over the top of the Nikon.

Clapping from the side of the set broke their eye contact. Frowning, Amanda turned.

Her colleague Nick stepped forward, still clapping. "That looked great."

"Yeah," Michelle said, speaking to Amanda. "I told you the camera would love you. Do you have time for a cup of coffee before I go process these pictures?"

"Sure. I have about twenty minutes while the crew sets up for the first take. I could show you around if you want."

Nick looked back and forth between them. "You two know each other?"

Michelle looked at Amanda before answering with a simple, "Yes."

"First time on a set?" Nick asked when no further explanation came. "Maybe one of the PAs can show you around while I steal Amanda for a second." He slung his arm around Amanda's shoulders and pulled her against his side.

Amanda struggled to free herself. "Can't this wait?"

"No. It's about today's first scene." He waved one of the production assistants over. "Hey, Cathy, can you show Amanda's friend the makeup trailer?" He gave Michelle a winning grin. "If you're lucky, they'll give you a fake head wound."

Michelle looked as if she wanted to give him a real one, but when more members of the cast and crew arrived on set, some of them vying for Amanda's attention, she finally said, "I'd better go break down my equipment. That head wound will have to wait. See you later. And break a leg in that first scene." She sent Amanda a long look that felt like a touch, slung her camera bag over her shoulder, and headed over to where her assistant had started packing up the equipment.

Amanda watched her go. *Damn.*

A knock on the door startled Amanda awake.

Disoriented, she sat up and rubbed her eyes. The script she had studied before dozing off slid from her chest and fell to the floor.

The knock on the trailer door came again.

"Yeah, yeah." She got up and opened the door.

A production assistant with a walkie-talkie around his neck stood on the top step. He held out a manila envelope. "This just came for you, Ms. Clark."

Amanda took the thick brown envelope. "What is it? Don't tell me more script changes."

"I don't think so. A messenger brought it over. Oh, and Mr. Bishop says to tell you he needs you back on stage three in half an hour." His walkie-talkie crackled to life, and he hurried away after a quick wave.

Amanda closed the door and trudged back to the couch. She studied the envelope with her name written on it in neat letters. Finally, she slid her finger beneath the flap and opened it. A stack of photographs fell into her lap. *The publicity shots. That was fast.*

Eagerly, she flipped through them. *Wow.* Maybe it was just Photoshop magic, but she looked great. Michelle had perfectly captured the intensity the producers had wanted for their crime-fighting detective, while at the same time posing her in a way that hinted at a vulnerability that would appeal to the audience.

Stuck to the last photo was a note, written in the same neat handwriting.

> *They turned out stunning, even if I do say so myself. But then again, it's hard to get a bad angle on a subject like you.*

Amanda smiled. "Charmer."

Then she spotted the post script beneath Michelle's signature.

> *P.S. As sexy as you look in your detective clothes and that leather jacket, I still want that private session.*

Laughing, Amanda reached for the phone to call her.

CHAPTER 11

"WHAT ARE YOU DOING HERE?" her grandmother greeted her when Amanda entered the kitchen.

Amanda bent to kiss her cheek. "Hello to you too. I'm spending my first afternoon off in forever with my much-missed grandmother, if you don't mind."

Her grandmother got up from the kitchen table, where she was poring over the crossword puzzle and drinking coffee—no doubt with a healthy splash of bourbon. "No, you're not."

"I'm not?"

"No."

"What else am I doing, then, oh mistress of my life and schedule?"

"You're gonna drive your cute little behind over to a certain bungalow in the Hollywood Hills and spend some time with a certain photographer who happens to have the afternoon off as well."

Amanda shook her head, directed her grandmother back into her chair, and sat next to her. "I can spend time with her later."

"Amanda Josephine Clark! Would you please go and spend the day with Michelle?"

"This coming from the woman who interrupted our first date!"

A hint of a blush dusted her grandmother's wrinkled face. "You are the one who always insists that it wasn't a date. Besides, I had to check her out to make sure she was right for you. You can't blame me for that."

"And you can't blame me for wanting to spend time with you."

Her grandmother pretended to study the crossword puzzle on the table. "Another word for stubborn with six letters. Hmm… Oh, right." In big, black letters, she filled in Amanda's name.

"I'm not being stubborn," Amanda said. "I just don't want you to think I'm neglecting you now that I'm in a relationship. My girlfriends have always had to accept that my job and my family come first."

"Maybe that's why they never worked out. No woman likes to play second or even third fiddle to an eighty-two-year-old and an acting gig."

Amanda shrugged. "Michelle has been very understanding so far."

"That girl is special. That's why you should hang on to her with both hands."

Memories returned of how she had clung to Michelle last week, holding on for just one more kiss until she had arrived in makeup ten minutes late. "Oh, I am hanging on to her; believe me."

Something in the tone of her voice made her grandmother look up from her crossword puzzle. A smile spread over her lined face. "I knew it! You're in love with her."

Amanda didn't try to deny it. Her grandmother knew her too well. "That doesn't mean I can't spend time with you."

"Lord, why did you have to inherit my stubbornness and not your grandfather's easygoing nature?"

Amanda laughed. "Just luck, I guess."

Her grandmother tugged on Amanda's chair as if wanting to wrench it out from under her. "Go. You can come back for dinner. And bring Michelle. I'm making her favorite."

"Hers, not mine?" Amanda pretended to pout.

Her grandmother shrugged. "I figure she'll need the energy to handle that stubborn granddaughter of mine."

"Thanks. I love you too."

"And I love you." Her grandmother caught her hand, squeezed it, and then let go. "And now go before we turn into two sentimental Hollywood divas."

After kissing her grandmother's cheek, Amanda rushed out the door and nearly skipped to her car. Full of glee at the prospect of spending the day with Michelle, she pressed number two on her cell phone's speed dial.

The phone rang and rang, and Amanda's elation dimmed. Usually, Michelle picked up her phone immediately if she wasn't at work. Maybe she was busy after all.

Just when Amanda thought voice mail would pick up any moment, Michelle's breathless voice came through the receiver. "Yes?"

Ridiculous how good just hearing her voice could make Amanda feel. "Hi. It's me."

No need to add a name. She knew Michelle would instantly recognize her voice, even if she hadn't looked at the caller ID.

"Oh, hi. Hang on a second." She talked to someone else, and the boisterous noises in the background ebbed away as if she had turned down the TV. Then Michelle was back. "Did the cameraman run out of film, or to what do I owe the pleasure of you calling me in the middle of the day?"

Amanda chuckled. "No, I'm afraid filming is all digital nowadays. But Detective Halliday is lazing around in a hospital bed after nearly being killed by a psychopath, so her partner gets to fight crime alone today and I get the afternoon off. My grandmother mentioned that you took the afternoon off too, so I thought this might be a good time to take those photos you mentioned." She glanced left and right to make sure she was alone. "You know, the ones with the sexy underwear."

"Damn."

Puzzled, Amanda stared at the phone for a second before moving it back to her ear. "You don't want to do that anymore?"

"Oh, yes." Michelle lowered her voice to a husky whisper. "You have no idea how much I want to do that, but..."

"Not a good time for you?"

"Not the best," Michelle said. "You're spoiling all the fun I had with the strippers."

"You!" Even though Michelle couldn't see it, Amanda threatened her with her index finger.

"Okay, okay, no strippers, but I do have three young ladies over."

Amanda frowned. "Are you still working?"

"No, I don't think my brother will pay me for this, although he really should."

"Your brother?"

"I'm babysitting my nieces."

At the word *babysitting*, protests came from somewhere in the background. "Oh, yeah, yeah, I know you're all grown-up and mature women of eight and ten. Pardon my mistake, ladies."

"Oh. I didn't know. Sorry. I didn't want to intrude on your time with—"

"You're not intruding," Michelle said immediately. "In fact, why don't you come over? We're about to head out for some ice cream and a movie, and we'd love to have you join us."

Amanda had never spent any time with children beyond playing a nanny in a movie once. But real life didn't have any stage directions, so she wasn't sure she would make a good babysitter. She didn't want to embarrass herself in front of Michelle or spoil her time with her nieces. "I don't know."

"Oh, come on. What do you say, kids? Do you want Amanda to come with us?"

Excited screams answered.

"See? They want you to come."

"They don't even know me."

"One more reason to come over and meet them," Michelle said. "My brother's misbehaving brood is a big part of my life, and I want you to get to know them." Her voice had lost its light, teasing tone.

Amanda swallowed. This meant a lot to Michelle, so she couldn't say no. Besides, Michelle had been more than wonderful to Amanda's grandmother, so she would suck it up and get over her nervousness around children. "All right. I'll come. Where should I meet you?"

"We'll pick you up at half past three."

She glanced at her wristwatch. Just enough time to make it home. "Okay."

"Thank you," Michelle said and hung up.

Amanda unlocked her car, sank into the driver's seat, and leaned her head against the steering wheel. Why did shooting a dozen takes of a kidnapping scene suddenly look like a pleasant activity compared to spending the afternoon with three little girls?

The excited chatter of the girls engulfed Amanda as soon as she got into the car. She closed the passenger-side door and turned to Michelle. "Hi," she said, unsure how to greet her in front of her nieces. Did the girls even know that their aunt was gay?

"Hi." Michelle leaned over and kissed her on the lips. Not a long, passionate smooch, but not just a quick peck on the cheek either.

Guess that answers that question.

"Girls," Michelle said, turning around to the backseat. "This is my girlfriend, Amanda."

Normally, Amanda thought the term *girlfriend* sounded a bit too juvenile for someone over thirty, but Michelle somehow managed to make it sound just right.

"Amanda, these are my nieces." She pointed at the girl in the middle, who seemed to be the oldest. "That's Hannah. And those are her sisters, Did Too and Did Not."

The two pigtailed girls giggled. "That's not my name, Aunt Mickey," one of them protested.

"It's not?" Michelle pretended to be stunned.

Amanda grinned broadly and lifted one eyebrow at her. "Aunt Mickey?"

"When the girls were little, they couldn't pronounce my name, so they called me Mickey instead. Somehow, the name stuck."

"It fits."

Michelle furrowed her brow. "Because it's butch?"

"You think the name Mickey is butch?" Laughing, Amanda shook her head. "It's cute, just like Mickey Mouse—and like you."

One of Michelle's eyebrows rose until it almost reached her hairline. "Cute?" she drawled.

Amanda fought the urge to lean over and kiss her. "Yes," she said. "Cute."

Her oldest niece stuck her head through the space between the seats and tugged on Michelle's sleeve. "Can we get going? We'll miss the movie."

"Aye, aye, ma'am." Michelle started the car and pulled away from the curb.

The scent of popcorn and hot dogs engulfed Amanda as soon as the glass doors swung open, starting a slideshow of happy memories of going to the movies with her grandmother as a child.

Michelle nudged her. "You look as happy as the three of them." She pointed to the girls.

"What can I say? I love the movies."

"Me too," one of the twins piped up. When she smiled up at Amanda, she looked so much like her aunt that it took Amanda's breath away for a moment.

The lobby of the movie theater was packed.

"Would you mind getting us some snacks while I get the tickets?" Michelle asked.

"No problem. I can do that. What would you like?"

"Whatever looks good to you," Michelle said. "I trust your judgment."

That little gesture meant a lot to Amanda. For some reason, when she had first gotten involved with Michelle, she had feared that Michelle would want to make all the decisions, but she wasn't like that at all.

"All right. Anything special for you girls?"

The twins and their older sister craned their necks to check out the snacks at the concession stand, but the crowd in the lobby blocked their view.

"I'll come with you and look at what they have," Hannah, the oldest, said.

"Me too," the twins shouted.

Uh-oh. Amanda sent Michelle a panicked glance. Leaving her alone with three kids was not a good idea. "Um, Michelle…"

Michelle just smiled and patted her arm. "They don't bite. Well, maybe Em and Nat do, but Hannah doesn't."

"Great. Come on, girls. Let's buy something unhealthy and fattening for your aunt."

As she got in line at the concession stand, the girls followed her like ducklings. The twins instantly started arguing about whether to get popcorn or nachos.

"You got to pick last time," one of them shouted.

"I did not."

"Did too."

Now Amanda knew why Michelle had introduced them that way. Before the battle over the movie theater snacks could escalate, she stepped between them. "You know what the good thing about going to the movies with so many people is?"

The girls looked up at her with big eyes. "What?"

"We don't need to decide. We'll just get nachos *and* popcorn." She wasn't above bribery to get into the girls' good graces.

"And chocolate?" Hannah asked.

"That too."

Loaded down with sodas, chocolate bars, a bucket of popcorn, and a large tray of nachos, they met Michelle at the other end of the lobby.

Michelle laughed when she saw them. "Did you leave anything for the other people?"

Amanda poked her in the ribs. "You're one to talk. Since you're such a fan of anything spicy, I bet you'll finish that tray of nachos all by yourself."

Grinning, Michelle ducked her head. "Guilty as charged, ma'am. I told you I like it spicy." She licked her lips and made a gimme-gimme motion in the direction of the nachos.

The twin who carried the nachos pulled them closer to her chest. "Oh, no, you won't."

"Don't worry," Amanda told her. "I'll sit between the two of you and make sure your aunt doesn't take more than her share."

"Thank you." The nacho twin latched on to Amanda's hand.

Startled, Amanda glanced down at the small fingers wrapped around her own and then up at Michelle, who smiled.

The usher ripped their tickets in half and handed them their slips. "Theater four is down the hallway to your right."

They headed down the hallway, juggled their junk food past rows of people, and took their seats.

Amanda watched as Michelle carefully helped the niece to her right slide her soda into the cup holder. She whispered something in the girl's ear, and Nat—or was it Em?—nodded enthusiastically.

She's a natural with kids. I wonder if she wants any of her own? The sudden thought freaked her out a little, but not as much as it had in the past, with some of her former partners. She could see herself settling down with Michelle, even if she wasn't sure yet about having kids.

Michelle looked up. Their gazes met.

"What?" Michelle patted her chest. "Do I have popcorn on my shirt? I know it can't be nachos, since the two of you aren't giving me any."

"Um, no, just wondering what movie we're watching," Amanda said. Now definitely wasn't the time to talk about having kids. It was too soon in their relationship for that topic anyway.

"*Rosey and the Fox*," one of the girls said.

Amanda nodded as if she had heard of that movie—which she of course hadn't. For someone in the acting business, she was woefully behind on industry news.

"It's an animated movie," Michelle said. "Sorry 'bout that."

"Oh, no. I love animated movies." At least she wouldn't think about camera angles and acting techniques while watching an animated movie.

Someone in the row behind them tapped Amanda on the shoulder.

She turned and gave the man and the boy next to him a questioning gaze.

"Excuse me, but are you Detective Halliday?" the man asked.

"Well, I play her on TV."

"Oh, yes, of course." The man beamed at her. "I'm a big fan. Would you mind taking a photo with me?"

Amanda had never before been approached by a fan. No wonder, since people usually didn't go gaga over commercials and one-time guest stars on daily soaps.

When she failed to answer, Michelle gently nudged her.

"Oh. Yes, of course."

The man handed his cell phone to the boy and turned so he could be photographed with Amanda.

"Let's do this in the aisle," Amanda said. "I don't want the girls to be in the photo."

People started turning their heads as Amanda and the man stepped into the aisle. Sweat broke out along Amanda's back, and she hoped no one else would ask for a photo or an autograph. For the first time, she wondered how big movie stars dealt with this constant attention from the public.

Finally, she took her seat again and leaned over to Michelle. "That was...weird."

"You'd better get used to it," Michelle said. "I have a feeling that will happen more often in the future. By the way, thanks."

"What for?"

"For protecting the girls from being photographed."

Amanda smiled. "You're welcome." Maybe she did have a bit of a maternal side after all.

The niece to her left tugged on Amanda's sleeve. "If you're a famous actress, do you have your own star?"

"Uh, no, I don't. I'm not that famous."

"Yet," Michelle said.

Again, their gazes met, and Amanda smiled, warmed by Michelle's trust in her acting skills.

"When I grow up, I'm gonna be an actress too," the girl next to Amanda said.

Michelle furrowed her brow. "Am I mistaken, or did you want to become a photographer just this morning, Em?"

Em shook her head. "Not anymore."

"There you have it." Michelle sighed deeply. "I think I lost my status as their favorite aunt."

Amanda shook her head. "I'm not their aunt."

Michelle winked at her with the eye that didn't have the scar. "Yet," she said again.

Michelle stopped the car in front of Amanda's apartment building and turned off the engine.

Despite her initial misgivings about spending the day with three kids, now Amanda didn't want it to end. "Want to come up? I have ice cream in my fridge, so we could have the ice cream you promised the girls right here."

"If you're sure your bachelorette pad can take the invasion of three preteens?"

"No worries. The couch wipes down."

"Hey, we're not babies," Hannah said with her bottom lip stuck out.

Michelle and Amanda exchanged smiles.

"Of course not," Amanda said.

They squeezed into the elevator, and Amanda enjoyed the warmth of Michelle's thigh against hers all the way to the top floor. When they reached her apartment, she handed out bowls of ice cream to the girls.

Michelle shook her head at the offer of ice cream. "No, thanks. I ate that bucket of popcorn almost by myself. If I eat anything else, I'm gonna be sick." She stood at the kitchen window and peered out. "I thought you had an ocean view?"

"I do. Come on; I'll show you." With one glance at the girls, who were busy devouring their ice cream, she took Michelle's hand and led her to the bedroom.

Michelle waggled her eyebrows. "Oooh, ocean view. I get it. Is that like having a stamp collection?"

Amanda slapped her arm. "No. Look." She moved to the window next to the bed, stood on her tiptoes, and craned her neck so she could see around the tanning salon and the twenty-four-hour pawn shop across the street.

After stepping next to her, Michelle did the same and laughed. "That tiny bit of blue in the distance is your ocean view?"

Amanda shrugged. "Hasn't anyone ever told you that size doesn't matter?"

"Is that so?" Michelle half-turned, wrapped both arms around Amanda, and bent her head to press a kiss to the sensitive spot right below Amanda's ear.

A shiver ran through Amanda, and she nearly lost her train of thought. "Yes. I admit the view is much nicer from the roof, though. Sometimes, after a really stressful day on the set, I climb up the fire escape and watch the sun set over the ocean."

"Hmm, that sounds nice. Will you show me one day?"

The rumbling sound of Michelle's humming sent more shivers through Amanda. Every cell of her body felt electrified with Michelle's closeness. "Yes." At that moment, she probably would have promised Michelle anything.

"Thank you." Michelle kissed that spot below her ear again and then nibbled and kissed her way across her jaw and her cheek, placing each kiss half an inch higher.

Impatient with her progress toward where she really wanted her, Amanda took her face between both hands and pressed their mouths together.

Passion instantly ignited and swept through Amanda like wildfire.

With a moan, she pressed closer, wanting more, wanting—

"Sssh." Breathing heavily, Michelle pulled away and touched her index finger to Amanda's lips. "Remember, we have three mini chaperones in the kitchen."

As the touch to her lips became a gentle stroking, Amanda couldn't resist one last kiss. "Will you have dinner with me and my grandmother tonight?" she asked when she finally put a respectable distance between them.

"I wish I could, but I promised my brother I'd take the girls overnight."

Amanda suppressed a sigh. "Maybe next weekend, then."

"Damn. I'm sorry, Mandy. I can't make it then either. It's my nephews' turn to stay with me." She groaned and let her head sink onto Amanda's shoulder.

Amanda slid her fingers through the short hair, enjoying its unexpected silkiness.

After a few moments, Michelle lifted her head and peered at her. "Oh, sorry. I just realized I called you Mandy."

"It's all right."

"I thought you didn't like that nickname?"

"I like it," Amanda said. "It just seemed too intimate when we barely knew each other."

Michelle studied her. "And now?"

Amanda kissed her again, this time not escalating the kiss, just connecting. "Now it feels just right."

One of the twins rushed into the bedroom. "Aunt Mickey, Emily ate all my ice cream."

"Did not," came the shout from the kitchen.

"Did too!"

"Did not. It was the cat."

Michelle wrapped her arm around Amanda's shoulders as if she needed to hold herself up. "Come on. I need to intervene before World War Three breaks out in your kitchen."

While the twins fought over who got to press the button for the elevator, Michelle turned back to Amanda. "So, when will I see you again?"

"I don't know. As far as I'm concerned, as soon as possible."

Michelle gave her a hopeful glance. "You don't, by any chance, want to spend next Sunday helping me babysit? I swear the boys are easier to handle."

"Are not," Emily shouted from the elevator.

"Are too." Michelle stuck her tongue out at her niece.

Amanda laughed. "All right, you two. No need to fight. If nothing comes up on the set, I'd love to help you babysit again. But this week could be pretty chaotic. It's our last week before we go on hiatus."

That reminded her... There would be a wrap party for the crew and cast on Friday, to celebrate the end of season two. Lorena had already said that she would bring her fiancé, and Nick was sure to have a woman or two hanging on his arms. Walt had invited her to bring someone too, but Amanda had escaped with a noncommittal answer, still not sure if making a public statement about her sexual orientation could hurt her career, now that it had finally started to take off.

For a moment, she was tempted to say to hell with it and just invite Michelle, but then she sighed and remained silent. Better not to rock the boat if you didn't know whether there were sharks in the water.

She gave Michelle a quick kiss and stood still, startled, as the girls hugged her good-bye. Then Michelle and her nieces were gone, and everything felt much too quiet after her noisy afternoon. She stood in the hallway, listening to the rattling of the elevator until she couldn't hear it anymore.

CHAPTER 12

ON HER WAY TO HER grandmother's, Amanda plugged in her cell phone and speed-dialed Kathryn. Absentmindedly, she realized that Michelle had replaced her agent as the number two on her speed dial.

"What can I do for my favorite actress today?" Kathryn said instead of a simple hi.

"You're not talking about my grandmother again, are you?"

Kathryn chuckled. "No. Since I get ten percent of what the studio is paying you, I'm definitely talking about you."

For the past four years, Kathryn had worked for ten percent of almost nothing, so Amanda didn't begrudge her the money. "I need some advice."

Kathryn instantly sobered. "I'm all ears."

"It's about Michelle."

"Oh, so this isn't about business after all. Well, I don't mind talking about your love life, but do you really think getting relationship advice from someone who's divorced three times is a good idea?"

"It is about business. Kind of." Amanda braked at a red light. "It's about the season wrap party on Friday. I'm thinking about taking Michelle."

Kathryn was silent for several seconds.

"Kath?"

"Yeah. Still here."

"You don't think that's a good idea."

The cars behind her started honking, and Amanda quickly crossed the intersection.

"I didn't say that. Not necessarily." Kathryn sighed. "But Hollywood is a fickle lady, and I don't want anything to spoil the success you've worked so hard for."

Amanda tightened her grip on the steering wheel. "My sexual orientation has nothing to do with my acting skills. It's not fair for anyone to judge me by that."

"I know. But since when has anything about show biz ever been fair?"

Silence spread between them, interrupted only by the tick-tock-tick-tock of the turn signal as Amanda made a turn left.

"I'm not saying don't take her to the party," Kathryn finally said. "Just...just think about it carefully before you make a decision like that, okay?"

Amanda had done little else since Walt had told her about the party. "Yeah. Thanks. I will." Maybe asking Kath for relationship advice really hadn't been the best of ideas. She said good-bye and ended the call, still none the wiser.

"Dig in," her grandmother said and piled more pasta onto Amanda's plate. "You're eating for two after all."

Amanda nearly inhaled a strand of spaghetti. "What?"

Her grandmother chuckled. "I didn't mean it like that—unless Michelle is more talented than I gave her credit for."

Speaking about her sex life with her grandmother was freaking her out, even if there was no sex life to speak of. She glared at her grandmother and continued to eat.

"I meant that you have to eat Michelle's portion too since she couldn't come to dinner." Grandma seemed almost as disappointed as Amanda about that.

Not having much of an appetite, Amanda slowly twirled a few strands of spaghetti around her fork. Her thoughts were still with Michelle and drifted from their afternoon at the movie theater to the wrap party. Calling Kathryn for advice hadn't helped her come to a decision.

Her grandmother watched her for a while. Finally, she covered Amanda's hand with her own, stopping her from twisting her fork around and around. "What is it? You and Michelle didn't have a fight, did you?"

"No. We're not spending enough time together to fight."

"Is that what has you so down?"

Amanda put her fork down. "I never thought it would be so hard to juggle a new role and a new relationship at the same time. I dreamed of landing a role like this for years, and now I'm starting to resent it for keeping me away from Michelle."

Her grandmother patted her hand. "Priorities change when you're in love. Just hang on until Friday, then you go on break and can see her all you want."

The thought of Friday didn't help to cheer Amanda up. "Did you ever take Grandpa to a wrap party?"

"Oh, no. Your grandfather hated parties, especially the parties thrown by Hollywood folks."

"Hmm." Amanda picked up her fork again and twirled it through the spaghetti without eating. Would Michelle even want to go? Maybe she was agonizing over nothing.

"Why are you asking?"

Without looking up from her plate, Amanda said, "I'm thinking about taking Michelle to the season wrap party on Friday."

"Oh, yes, take her. I bet that girl is the life of every party. She gets along with people so well. The ladies at bridge night loved her."

That made Amanda look up. "You took her to bridge night?"

"When you were in Vegas for a week, she was lonely, so I occasionally asked her over to watch TV and play cards."

Amanda nearly laughed out loud. Michelle and her grandmother had searched out each other's company, each claiming that the other one was lonely. *Too cute.* It was amazing how well Michelle fit into her private life; if only it were that easy to reconcile their relationship with her job.

"So it's decided, then," her grandmother said. "You'll take her to the party."

"It's not that easy. If I take her to the party, everyone will know I'm gay."

Her grandmother studied her across the table and then stood and pulled Amanda up. "Let's go to the living room and have a talk."

It had been this way since Amanda's childhood. All serious talks took place in the living room, with her grandmother sitting in her armchair and Amanda perched on the ottoman. This had been the spot where Amanda had come out to her grandmother and where she had learned that her grandfather had terminal cancer.

When they were seated, her grandmother took her hand. "What's going on with you, Mandy? You were never afraid to be out."

"I never had anything to lose. Mom and Dad had already disinherited me when I moved here, so I had no reason to be in the closet, but now I have a career to worry about."

"Do you really think being gay will be an issue?" her grandmother asked.

"I don't know," Amanda said, looking down at her grandmother's age-spotted hand, entwined with her own. "And I'm not in a hurry to find out. Do you remember what Lennard, my first agent, told me?"

"That bloodthirsty shark?"

"He might be a shark, but he knows the business. He said that if you want to make it in show biz, you can't afford to have a private life—and certainly not if you're gay. Kath also thinks it's better to be careful and not rock the boat right now."

Her grandmother's silver-gray brows pinched together. "Pardon my language, but that's a pile of horse poop. I had a career in show biz before Kathryn and Lennard even knew how to spell Hollywood, and the only reason why I could have that career was that I had a private life to balance it. I never would have survived thirty years as an actress without your grandfather."

Amanda didn't doubt it for a second. "Yes, but you're not gay. What if I come out to my colleagues, and soon, producers and casting directors start thinking that they can't cast me in romantic comedies or family-oriented movies because their audience wouldn't like it or they think that I can't believably pretend to be in love with a man?"

Her grandmother thought about it for a moment. "It's a risk," she finally admitted. "But, Mandy, this Hollywood business… It's not real. All the really important things in life happen off-screen. What good does all the fame, glamor, and money do if you can't be yourself? It's hard enough not losing yourself when you're playing a different role every few months. You shouldn't have to pretend to be someone else when the cameras are off."

She felt the truth of those words as soon as her grandmother said them. During those crazy days on the set, her daily phone calls with Michelle had kept her grounded. What good would it do to build a career, get bigger roles, until she might one day even win an Emmy or an Oscar, when she couldn't even thank Michelle in the acceptance speech?

Amanda stood and kissed her grandmother's cheek. "Thank you." She strode toward the door.

"Where are you going?"

"To get my cell phone from the kitchen. I have to call Michelle and invite her to the party."

"Are the monsters in bed?"

Michelle chuckled. "Out like a light. Guess spending the day with a celebrity tired them out."

"I'm not a celebrity."

"Not yet," Michelle said, as Amanda had known she would. "But they liked you anyway."

"They did?" That meant more to Amanda than she had known. "Really?"

"Sure. They inherited their aunt's good taste when it comes to women."

Amanda couldn't help laughing. "Goof. Listen, I called for a reason." She lowered her voice, even though her grandmother had stayed behind in the living room to give her some privacy. "I want to invite you to our season wrap party on Friday. I know you have to babysit your nephews on Saturday, but would you want to go with me if I promise not to keep you out too late?"

"Of course," Michelle said without even a hint of hesitation. "My brother won't drop off my nephews before noon on Saturday anyway. But...won't your colleagues wonder why you're dragging a photographer to a cast party?"

"I won't be bringing a photographer," Amanda said. "I'll be bringing my girlfriend."

Michelle sucked in an audible breath. "Are you sure that's what you want to do? You could just introduce me as a friend, if that would be easier for you."

Amanda clamped her hand around the phone more tightly. "I'm sure," she said despite the nervous flutter in her stomach.

"All right. Tell me when, and I'll be there to pick you up, dressed up worthy of accompanying the rising star of prime-time TV."

"Seven o'clock."

"It's a date."

"Yes," Amanda said. "This time, it is."

CHAPTER 13

MICHELLE WAS TEN MINUTES EARLY, but Amanda had been waiting for twenty minutes already, filled with nerves about coming out to her colleagues and the anticipation of seeing Michelle again.

She leaned in the doorway of her apartment when the elevator doors pinged open.

Greedily, she drank in the sight of Michelle in a midnight blue dress shirt and black pants that showed off her muscular legs.

Michelle's steps faltered when she caught sight of her.

Amanda looked down at herself. "Do you think I'm overdressed?"

"Uh, no. You look…" She stopped in front of Amanda and exhaled sharply. "Stunning." Her eyes smoldered as she took in Amanda's black, one-shouldered dress and the amount of skin it left bare.

"So do you." Amanda gave in to the temptation to touch the shirt and find out if it was as satiny smooth as it looked. But as soon as she touched Michelle's shoulder and felt the heat radiating off her, she forgot about the shirt and slid her arms around her.

As their bodies touched, Michelle seemed to sway a little. She groaned. "You do know that wearing this dress is cruel, when all I want is to take it off you, don't you?"

Heat flared through Amanda at her words and the hoarse sound of her voice. Unable to answer, she just took Michelle's hand and pulled her into the apartment before they ended up giving the neighbors a show. *Again.* She kicked the door closed.

They stood close in the narrow hall of the apartment, and Amanda became aware that she was alone with Michelle in what felt like the first time in weeks. That thought sent a tingle of anticipation through her.

Michelle cleared her throat and fumbled with the top button of her shirt as if the collar were suddenly too tight. "Ready to go?"

Amanda was tempted to just stay in, but she nodded instead. "Yeah, I just need my purse." When she turned and took a step down the hall to get the purse, the slit in her dress parted, revealing a glimpse of her thigh.

Michelle let out another groan. "Jesus."

Smiling to herself, Amanda looked over her shoulder. "Something wrong?"

"Oh, no. Something's very, very right," Michelle murmured and moved closer. She pressed her lips to the top of Amanda's bare shoulder blade and trailed one fingertip up the slit in her dress, caressing the back of her thigh.

Amanda's breath caught. Her heart skipped a beat and then started hammering double-time as Michelle began to kiss every inch of exposed skin along her back. A nip to her shoulder made her knees go weak, so she caught herself with both hands against the wall. "If you don't stop what you're doing, we'll never make it to the party," she whispered, barely recognizing her own voice.

"What am I doing?" Michelle slid the strap of fabric farther down Amanda's shoulder. Her breath fanned over Amanda's skin with every word, sending shivers down the rest of her body.

"Driving me crazy."

Breathing heavily, Michelle pressed closer. Her left hand, the one that wasn't caressing her thigh, slid around Amanda's hip and came to rest just below her belly button. "Hmm. Good. Because you do the same to me."

Amanda lost all ability to answer or even to think. Instead, she turned around and kissed her hungrily.

They crashed into the coatrack but didn't stop kissing.

Michelle pressed her against the wall and slid one leg between the slit in Amanda's dress, rubbing against her in a way that made Amanda's head spin.

Amanda moaned and pulled Michelle's shirttails out of her pants, desperate to touch her bare skin. "Bedroom."

"What about…" Michelle nipped one bare shoulder, "…the party?"

"Forget the damn party."

Michelle smiled against Amanda's shoulder but still hesitated. "Are you sure? You said you wanted more than just a quickie."

"I do," Amanda said, exploring the smooth, muscular plane of Michelle's back. "And we will have more. Later. But now, I really need…this. I need you."

Michelle enclosed her mouth with a passionate kiss the second she'd finished speaking. "I need you too," she whispered hoarsely against her lips. She started walking backward without letting go of Amanda, pulling her with her to the bedroom.

When Michelle's back hit the bedroom door, Amanda fumbled for the doorknob with one hand while exploring the skin of Michelle's lower back with the other.

Finally, she got the door open.

Tearing at each other's clothes, they stumbled toward the bed.

Instead of throwing her onto the bed, as Amanda had halfway expected, Michelle slowed things down. She trailed one finger over the fabric of Amanda's dress. "Hmm, maybe you are overdressed after all." Inch by inch, she slid the dress's strap down Amanda's shoulder and bared the top of her breasts.

Amanda's nipples tightened, aching to be touched.

"No bra?" Michelle asked, her voice rough.

Amanda shook her head. This dress didn't allow for a bra, and now she was glad about it. One fewer article of clothing to get rid of.

With a hum of appreciation, Michelle bent and kissed the bare skin of her collarbone, then let her lips wander down to her cleavage, nuzzling into her. Her hands trailed down Amanda's back, finding the zipper of the dress and slowly lowering it.

The rasp of the zipper sounded loud to Amanda's sensitized ears. She struggled to get out of the dress and into Michelle's arms.

As the dress slid down, Michelle followed its path with her lips, kissed down her breasts, circled the areola, and finally flicked her warm tongue over one nipple.

Jolts of pleasure shot through Amanda's body. "Oh God. Bed. Now." After kicking off her high heels and the dress pooling around her feet, she sank onto the bed and shivered at the contrast of the cool sheets below her and Michelle's heat covering her.

Without taking the time to undress first, Michelle instantly began making love to every inch of Amanda's body. She kissed a path along her clavicles and then dipped her tongue into the hollow between. Her fingertips trailed up and down Amanda's sides, brushing her breasts, as she slowly lowered her mouth to one of Amanda's nipples again.

Gasping, Amanda wove her fingers through Michelle's short hair and pressed her head closer against herself.

Michelle nibbled, flicked, and sucked. When Amanda started squirming, she rasped her teeth gently over the hardened nipple.

Amanda's back arched, and she pressed into Michelle's mouth. Her body burned wherever Michelle's lips and hands touched her.

Never moving away from Amanda's breasts, Michelle slid one of her hands lower. Her fingertips drifted along the edges of her black panties.

"Yes." Amanda shifted her hips, inviting Michelle to touch. "Please."

Still caressing Amanda's breast with her lips, Michelle slid her hand down and into Amanda's panties. "Oh God, Amanda." Michelle's pupils dilated until her eyes looked nearly black. She circled Amanda's clit with one finger.

A buzzing sound started in Amanda's ears. She bucked against Michelle's hand, wanting her closer, harder, faster.

Instead, Michelle moved back. Before Amanda could protest, she kissed down her body until the edge of the panties stopped her. With gentle fingers, she stripped them off. She leaned over Amanda, staring down at her with an intense gaze. Her shirt was halfway unbuttoned, but otherwise, she was still fully dressed.

There was something strangely erotic about being completely naked while her partner still had all of her clothes on. Amanda clutched her shoulders, pulling her down, and crushed their mouths together with an intensity that robbed them both of breath.

When Michelle slid her hand between them and down her belly, Amanda moaned into her mouth.

Holding herself up on one hand, Michelle gently massaged Amanda's clit between the V of her fingers.

A ball of tension gathered low in Amanda's belly. She writhed against Michelle and broke their kiss to gasp for breath. "More. More."

Michelle flicked one fingertip directly over her clit. Then, when Amanda was just about to go insane, she slid her fingers lower and entered her.

"God, yes." Amanda dug her nails into Michelle's muscled buttocks and moved against her fingers. Moaning helplessly, she buried her face against Michelle's shoulder. The muscles in her thighs started to tremble, and she couldn't keep her eyes open any longer. She tried to hang on and prolong the feelings coursing through her, but when Michelle skated her thumb across her clit, she shattered.

Every muscle in her body tensed and then went limp. She fell back onto the bed, still clutching Michelle's ass.

Michelle rolled them around and settled Amanda more comfortably against her shoulder. After letting her rest for a minute, she pulled back her fingers, lifted her head, and kissed Amanda tenderly.

Amanda slipped her fingers into Michelle's hair and pulled her closer as the kiss became more passionate.

With a groan, Michelle pulled away and glanced at the alarm clock on Amanda's bedside table. "The party." She tried to slip out from under Amanda. "We really need to get—"

"Oh, no." Amanda straddled her hips and pressed her back down. "I'm not a pillow queen. Lie still and let me love you."

Trapped beneath Amanda, Michelle stared up at her and then barked out a startled laugh. That laugh turned into a moan as Amanda bent and lightly bit her neck.

Amanda slid her hands into the half-open shirt. Heat radiated off Michelle's flushed skin. "Now you are the overdressed one."

When Michelle lifted shaking hands to unbutton her shirt, Amanda shook her head.

"No. Let me."

Michelle let her arms flop to the bed, palms up as if surrendering herself.

The gesture was a powerful aphrodisiac. Amanda pressed herself against Michelle and moaned at the friction of Michelle's pants against her still sensitive clit. *No. Not this time. This is for her.*

She lifted up a bit so she could focus on undressing Michelle. In her impatience, she was tempted to just rip off the buttons but forced herself to go slow and enjoy every moment.

Finally, the fabric parted, revealing a sleeveless T-shirt that molded to her strong shoulders.

"That too," Amanda said, already breathless at the thought of Michelle's skin against her own.

Michelle sat up with Amanda still straddling her, and they struggled to free her of the T-shirt.

Amanda threw it on the heap of clothes next to the bed, never taking her gaze off Michelle.

She wasn't wearing a bra either. She didn't need one since her breasts were smaller than Amanda's.

A perfect handful. Amanda's mouth watered. She slid lower on the bed and licked a hot path down Michelle's neck and chest, enjoying the saltiness of her skin. When she reached her breasts, she circled first one, then the other like an ice cream cone, making the circles smaller and smaller until she finally sucked one nipple into her mouth.

Michelle thrashed against her but kept her hands pressed to the bed, as if Amanda had shackled them there. Gasps and moans and something that almost sounded like a prayer fell from her lips.

Amanda massaged the other breast with her hand. *Oh. She's so sensitive.* She watched the pleasure on Michelle's face as she continued to caress her breasts with her hands and her mouth. Strong thighs and muscled hips arched beneath her, pressing against her own wetness and making her gasp.

She had wanted to tease Michelle a little, but finally she was the one who couldn't stand it any longer, so she moved lower, kissing down a flat belly and exploring the bands of muscles with her lips and tongue. In the past, she had preferred womanly curves and softness, but now Michelle's strong body was a huge turn-on.

Slowly, she unbuckled Michelle's leather belt and pulled it free before sliding the pants down her long legs, taking unexpected pleasure in undressing her. For a moment, she sat back and admired the contrast between the boxer shorts and the smooth skin of Michelle's legs; then she couldn't stand the inches of space between them anymore. She helped her out of the boxers and slid between Michelle's thighs. Her nostrils flared as she breathed in her musky scent. Again trailing kisses down Michelle's chest and belly, she moved lower on the bed.

Weakly, Michelle lifted her head and looked down at her. "You don't have to—"

Amanda lifted one hand and laid her index finger against her own lips in a shushing gesture. Without saying a word, she bent her head and kissed the inside of a smooth thigh. She stopped when she reached her damp, dark curls.

Michelle arched upward, silently asking for her touch.

With a gentle nudge, Amanda directed her to lift one leg over her shoulder and dipped her tongue into the wet heat.

They both moaned at the same time.

Amanda barely brushed along the outer folds, circled the stiff clit without really touching it, and teased her with a few quick flicks of her tongue.

"Oh, Christ. You're..." Michelle gulped in a mouthful of air, "...killing me."

Taking mercy on her, Amanda swiped her tongue more firmly over her clit and then pressed closer and sucked it into her mouth.

Michelle clutched the bedding with both hands and rolled her head from side to side on the pillow. Tremors began to ripple through her, and a slow pulsing started against Amanda's tongue. Michelle's hips bucked uncontrollably.

Amanda slid one hand beneath her and clutched her ass, keeping her pressed against her. Slowly, guided by Michelle's rhythm, she increased her sucking and reached up to massage one breast.

With a shout, Michelle threw her head back. Her body arched up and then went taut and dropped back against the bed.

One last swipe of Amanda's tongue evoked a shudder.

Michelle let go of the bedding and tugged on Amanda's shoulder. "Come up here," she said, her voice hoarse.

Amanda slid back up, enjoying the brush of Michelle's sweat-dampened body against hers. She settled down half on top of Michelle, one leg tucked between her thighs.

Michelle wrapped her arms around her. After blinking a few times, as if she had trouble focusing her eyes, she just looked at Amanda. Tenderly, she combed a strand of hair behind one of Amanda's ears and then leaned up to kiss her, keeping eye contact until the very last moment, when their lips met.

Tingles shot down Amanda's body, and she was instantly ready for more.

"You're incredible," Michelle said, her voice still raspy. "I've never let anyone top me like that before."

"I didn't top you."

Michelle smiled and tapped Amanda's nose. "Oh, yeah, you did."

"Did not." Amanda rolled off Michelle and flopped onto the bed next to her. Laughing, she peered over at her. "God, we're beginning to sound like your nieces. I think we better get our asses to the party."

Michelle jumped out of bed. "Race you to the shower."

For a moment, the sight of Michelle's sculpted body distracted her. Visions of rubbing against that body in the shower and having those talented hands lathering soap all over her flashed through her mind. She shook her head to clear it. "Oh, no. We're taking turns in the shower, or we'll never get out of here."

On shaky legs, she stalked past Michelle and forced herself to close the bathroom door between them. While she waited for the water to heat up, she clutched the sink with both hands and stared at herself in the mirror. Except for the bedhead and her flushed cheeks, she looked the same as always, although she felt transformed by the experience of being with Michelle.

"Oh, wow," she whispered and then wrenched her gaze away from her image in the mirror and stepped beneath the warm spray.

CHAPTER 14

"Ah, you finally made it," Lorena said when they joined her and her fiancé at the buffet table. "Fashionably late, like a true star."

Amanda felt her cheeks turn nine shades of red. "We got caught in traffic," she murmured, figuring traffic always made for a good excuse in LA.

"Oh, I bet you got caught in something all right." Lorena winked and gave Michelle a long glance, letting her gaze slide over her from her polished loafers to her slightly disheveled hair. "Don't you want to introduce me to your boyfr—" She did a double-take. "Your, uh..."

"My girlfriend," Amanda said. "Michelle Osinski."

After a few seconds, Lorena stopped staring and shook Michelle's hand. She looked from Michelle to Amanda. "So you're...?"

"Gay. Yes." Amanda forced herself to stand tall and not fidget under her colleague's curious gaze.

"Does Nick know? I got the feeling he has a thing for you."

Amanda sighed as she caught movement over Lorena's shoulder. "He'll know in about twenty seconds. He's headed this way."

Nick joined them carrying two cocktail glasses. "Hey, there you are." He sounded as if he had already had a few of whatever drink he was holding. "I was beginning to think you were standing me up."

Standing him up? Amanda exchanged a quick glance with Michelle. "This is a wrap party, Nick, not a date."

"Details, details. Here." He held out one of the drinks toward Amanda. "I thought you could use a screaming orgasm."

Making good use of her acting skills, Amanda held back a smirk. *Thanks, I already had one tonight.* She jumped and grinned when Michelle pinched her butt behind her colleagues' backs. "No, thanks," she said to Nick. "I gave up drinking vodka. It makes me do stupid things."

"I don't know," Michelle said, her low voice rumbling through Amanda from right behind her. "Some of those stupid things turned out pretty well."

Amanda turned and smiled at her. For a moment, she forgot the party and her colleagues, who were watching her, as she looked into Michelle's eyes. "Yes, they did."

Michelle took her hand, lifted it to her lips, and kissed it.

Nick nearly spilled his cocktails all over himself. "Amanda? I thought the photographer is just a friend? What the hell is going on?"

"Oh, get a clue, Nick." Lorena rolled her eyes at him. "Amanda's a lesbian, and I don't mean that in the Britney Spears way, so do us all a favor and finally stop asking her out."

While Nick stood gaping, Walt came over with the show's executive producer and the head writer in tow.

Amanda swallowed as she was faced with the show's powers that be. Michelle's hand seemed to burn in her own, but she refused to let go.

But the three men either didn't notice them holding hands or chose to ignore it.

Walt looked from Michelle to Lorena's fiancé. "If you'd excuse us, we need to kidnap our stars for a minute. There's something important we have to talk about."

That sounded ominous. What was going on? A lump formed in Amanda's throat. The show wasn't going to be canceled, was it? The ratings were spectacular. But what else could be so important that they needed to drag their lead actors away from the wrap party?

Michelle gave her hand an encouraging squeeze before letting go. "I'll be right here."

David, the executive producer, led them to a back room and gestured toward a conference table. "I think you'd better sit down."

Uh-oh. It couldn't be good news, then, could it? With weak knees, Amanda sank onto one of the leather chairs and exchanged worried glances with Lorena and Nick.

Walt settled across the table from them. "No need to look so worried. This is all good. At least I think it is. We've already been renewed for a third season, and our ratings are better than we ever dreamed of, especially in the eighteen to thirty-four age group."

Amanda slumped against the back of the chair and exhaled. So the show wasn't being canceled. Far from it. What was this impromptu little meeting about, then?

"Which is why we think we should open the new season with a bang," Ron, the head writer, said and slid clipped stacks of red pages across the table.

"That's what I've been saying all along," Nick said. "We need bigger action scenes and—"

"Not according to our ratings," David, the executive producer said. "They're always best when we air one of the episodes with a more personal story. This is why we think we can get away with this." He nodded down at the script.

Amanda stared at the red pages, almost afraid to touch them. She had heard of top-secret scripts that were printed on red paper so no one could photocopy them, but she had never seen one so far.

"Go ahead and take a look," David said.

Hesitantly, Amanda picked up the stack of paper in front of her and started reading. The first page held the episode's title, "Gamble." *Ah.* So it was probably about her character's gambling addiction. *I can do that.* Especially now that she craved Michelle as a starving person craved food, her portrayal of a woman struggling with addiction should be Oscar-worthy.

More relaxed now, she flipped through the pages, reading some passages here and there, and quickly became engrossed in the story. In this episode, Detective Halliday's father, who'd made an appearance on the show before, was murdered and landed on the medical examiner's table.

"Great." Lorena sighed. "Amanda gets the interesting scenes, playing the grieving daughter, while I get to cut open bodies." Despite her complaints, she gave Amanda a smile.

"Oh, don't worry; it gets pretty interesting for you too," Ron said. "You might want to flip to page thirty-eight. That's the start of the sequence of scenes between your character, Lorena, and yours, Amanda."

So the show's female characters, Detective Halliday and Dr. Roberta Castellano, were finally getting more airtime. So far, Amanda's character had interacted mostly with her partner, played by Nick.

Dave looked from Amanda to Lorena. "We need you and your agents to okay that storyline before we start shooting in August."

Why did Kath need to okay the script? With trembling fingers, Amanda opened the script to page thirty-eight and began to read.

```
INT. MEDICAL EXAMINER'S OFFICE —
AUTOPSY ROOM — DAY

Dr. Roberta Castellano bends over
Jack Halliday's body on the cold
metal slab and lifts her hand with
the scalpel when Detective Linda
Halliday enters the autopsy room.
Castellano puts the scalpel down
```

and quickly covers the body with
a sheet.

> CASTELLANO
> What are you
> doing here?

> HALLIDAY
> My job.

Castellano shakes her head and
rounds the gurney to stand in front
of her.

> CASTELLANO
> This isn't about the
> job. He's your father.
> You shouldn't be here.

> HALLIDAY
> I have to do something.

Castellano takes another step forward
and touches Halliday's hand.

> CASTELLANO
> I know how you feel.

Halliday looks down, torn between wanting to lean into the touch and wanting to be strong. After a few seconds, she jerks her hand away.

> HALLIDAY
> Like hell you do.

> CASTELLANO
> Yes, I do. I lost my partner almost the same way three years ago.

> HALLIDAY
> I'm sorry.
> (beat)
> Your…partner?

A small smile curls Castellano's lips, but it doesn't quite reach her eyes.

> CASTELLANO
> Not in the cop sense, Detective. She was my wife. Or she would have been if the law had been different back then.

Amanda stopped reading and looked up from the script. When she turned her head, she met Lorena's startled gaze.

"I'm gay?" Lorena asked, looking from David to Ron and Walt. "I mean…my character is?"

Ron nodded. "I hope you're okay with it." He glanced at Amanda. "Both of you. Because if you turn to the last page…"

Amanda did.

```
INT. CASINO — NIGHT


Detective Halliday walks up to the
poker table with a stack of chips and
is just about to sit down. CLOSE-
UP on a hand covering Halliday's,
holding her back. Halliday turns.


          CASTELLANO
     Don't do this.


           HALLIDAY
     Why shouldn't I? I
     lost my father, we
     lost the trial against
     his murderer… I have
     nothing left to lose.
```

<pre>
                    CASTELLANO
              (whispering)
         You didn't lose me.

Halliday stares at her.

                    HALLIDAY
         You mean...?

Castellano nods, steps forward, and
kisses her. Halliday drops her stack
of chips and returns the kiss.

                         FADE TO BLACK.

         END OF EPISODE.
</pre>

Amanda put the script down, stared at Lorena, and tried to imagine kissing her. Lorena had been on the "sexiest women alive" list of several magazines in the last two years and was just the curvy, feminine type that Amanda usually went for, but now the thought of kissing her on camera was about as appealing as shooting that kidnapping scene in the cabin all over again—maybe because there was nothing sexy about shooting kiss scenes with all the cameras, technicians, and makeup artists around, or maybe because all she wanted was to leave the party and kiss Michelle instead.

"What the hell...?" Nick threw down the script with so much force that it skidded across the table and dropped to the floor.

"This isn't just a sweeps month stunt, is it?" Lorena asked, narrowing her eyes at the head writer.

Ron shook his head. "No. We want to do what the powers that be should have done in *Law and Order: SVU*."

"Risk our ratings crashing?" Nick mumbled.

"Have a lesbian main character in a prime-time TV show," Ron said without looking at him. "This is your chance to expand your repertoire, Lorena. You've been asking us to write a little romance for Dr. Castellano into the script." He shrugged. "But if you're not okay with this..."

"I didn't say that." Lorena traced the front page of the script with her fingertips. "I didn't expect this, but it's well written." She straightened and grinned at Nick, who sat with his arms crossed over his chest. "At least one of us will get to kiss Amanda."

David turned toward Amanda. "I assume you're fine with it? Not to sound indelicate, but you know Hollywood people can't keep a secret to save their lives, so we know you've got...previous experience."

Amanda nearly fell off her chair. All this agonizing, all those sleepless nights over the decision to come out to her colleagues, and the show's producer, head writer, and director had known all along?

"I'm fine with it," she finally managed to say.

"Good." David started gathering scripts. "I'll need to check with your agents, of course, but we'd really like to go through with this."

Amanda still stared at the three men.

Lorena nudged her. "Come on. Let's get out of here before Nick convinces them to make it a threesome."

Still in a daze, Amanda stumbled out of the conference room. The noise of the party engulfed her, and she scanned the crowd, looking for Michelle. She finally found her on the other side of the room, talking to one of the cameramen and sipping from a bottle of beer.

As if sensing Amanda looking at her, Michelle lifted her head, and their gazes met. Michelle immediately excused herself from the conversation. With a few quick steps, she was at Amanda's side and slung one arm around her. "Hey, you okay? You look a bit..."

"Shell-shocked," Amanda said.

"What's going on? They didn't fire you or anything, did they?" Michelle looked as if she was ready to storm over to the person responsible for such a decision and rip off his head.

Amanda shook her head. "No."

"What is it, then?"

"Remember when I was joking about doing a little bondage play with Lorena?"

Michelle's eyebrows pinched together. "Yeah."

"Well, it seems I'll really get to do that."

Michelle nearly dropped the bottle of beer she was holding. "What?"

Amanda took the beer from her and took a thoroughly needed swig. "Well, maybe not the bondage, but they wrote a lesbian storyline into season three. The first episode will end with a lip-lock between Lorena and me—or rather between Dr. Castellano and Detective Halliday."

"Wow." Michelle took the bottle back and emptied it with a few big gulps. "I don't know if I should be jealous or aroused. Probably both."

"Neither. Believe me, there's nothing sexy about shooting a kiss scene. How would you like kissing a co-worker while the entire crew is watching and a big, burly guy is holding a light over you?"

"Not my idea of a hot night," Michelle said. She put the empty beer bottle down on a table and grasped Amanda's hand. "Well, there are no big, burly guys with lights in your bedroom, but how about we go home and rehearse?"

Amanda didn't have to be asked twice. After all, practice did make perfect.

Amanda woke at sunrise, pleasantly sore in all the right places. She stretched languidly and smiled at the memories of last night. Despite getting just three hours of sleep, she felt great. When she rolled around to cuddle up to Michelle, she realized that the bed next to her was empty.

Frowning, she sat up. For a moment, she wondered if she'd dreamed everything. It certainly wouldn't be the first time she'd had vivid dreams about making love to Michelle.

But Michelle's scent surrounded her, and the midnight blue dress shirt she'd worn last night still lay next to the bed, where Amanda had stripped it off Michelle, nearly ripping the buttons.

A gust of wind from the partially open window formed goose bumps on Amanda's bare skin. She reached for the pair of sweatpants lying on the chair next to the bed and slipped into Michelle's shirt, inhaling the scent of her cologne as she buttoned it up halfway.

Then she went in search of her missing lover.

The ladder on the fire escape was down, giving her a good idea of where Michelle had gone.

Amanda climbed out of the window and onto the fire escape and carefully made her way up to the roof.

Michelle was sitting on the folding chair Amanda kept up there, barefoot, wearing just her pants and the sleeveless T-shirt. The silky material stretched across her strong shoulders.

Immediately, Amanda wanted to drag her down the fire escape and back to bed. "I see you found my ocean view."

Michelle turned. Her eyes lit up. "Yes. But I like this view much better." She slid her gaze over the shirt, which hung a little too low on Amanda, revealing a good bit of cleavage. "I hope you don't mind me coming up here without you. You were sleeping so peacefully, and I didn't want to wake you since you rarely get a chance to sleep in."

"It's okay. My roof is your roof. I want you to feel at home in my apartment."

"I do." Michelle reached out and pulled Amanda onto her lap.

Humming, Amanda snuggled closer. She kissed Michelle's cheek, then the scar at the corner of her eye before leaning against her shoulder.

Neither spoke as they watched the city wake up far below.

Finally, when the gray light of dawn gave way to the hazy blue of a Los Angeles morning, Michelle guided Amanda's head around to look into her eyes. "Thank you for last night."

"You're thanking me? I should be thanking you—repeatedly." Amanda fanned herself with both hands. "Last night was incredible."

Michelle smiled. "Yes, it was. But I was talking about you taking me to the wrap party. I know what this role means to you, and I'm sure a few months ago, you couldn't even imagine risking it for someone like me."

"True. Falling in love with you was a departure from the script in the best possible way."

Michelle stilled beneath her. Even her breathing stopped for a moment. Then she sucked in a breath. "Did you just say...?"

Amanda hadn't meant to just blurt it out without thought. She had wanted to make it special and romantic. Then again, sharing this morning high up on the roof with Michelle was special and romantic. "That I love you. Yes. I hope I didn't leave any doubt about it last night."

"Hmm." Michelle's hands made their way beneath the shirt. "I might need a reminder."

"Oh, yeah? Do I need to—?"

In the apartment below them, the phone began to ring.

Amanda groaned and buried her head against Michelle's shoulder. "Christ. What is it with us and phone calls that keep interrupting at the most inopportune of times?" When the answering machine clicked on and her grandmother's voice drifted up through the open window, she moved to get up from Michelle's lap.

Michelle didn't let go. "I have no idea, but I'm not moving an inch until I tell you…" she tipped Amanda's chin up with one finger so she could look her in the eyes, "…that I love you too."

Their lips met in a long, slow kiss full of promises for the future. Then Amanda got up, took Michelle's hand, and pulled her inside for more rehearsal. She could call her grandmother back later. Much, much later.

EPILOGUE

As they were about to enter the eighth store, her grandmother dug in her heels like a stubborn mule and refused to move another inch. "I love shopping as much as the next actress, but this is ridiculous. You'd think you were trying to decide on a wedding ring. It's a Valentine's Day card, Mandy!"

"I know, but it can't be just any Valentine's Day card. I need something special."

The salesclerk walked over. "Is there a problem, ladies? We have all sorts of cards. I'm sure you'll find something." He paused and squinted at Amanda, who tensed.

She had seen that squint a lot in the past few months. "Wait a minute! Aren't you...?"

Amanda's grandmother patted his hand. "Oh, we get that a lot. Doesn't she look just like that woman who won an Emmy for playing that detective on TV?"

"Yeah." The salesclerk still looked at Amanda and shook his head. "Amazing resemblance. They could be twins."

"No. I'm her grandmother, so I know for a fact that she doesn't have any siblings."

Amanda was about to retreat before he realized they had tricked him when she caught sight of a card that had been relegated to an out-of-the-way corner of the rack of Valentine's Day cards. "This! This is it." She reached for the card and waved it triumphantly.

Her grandmother took her glasses out of her purse and studied the card. "Uh, Mandy, dear, I'm beginning to think you inherited your grandfather's rather...um...endearing taste in holiday cards."

Amanda had to admit that the card with the picture of Cupid, an arrow piercing his back between his pristine, white wings, might not appear the most romantic to anyone else, but if not for a flyer with the picture of this little guy, they would have never met. "Michelle will understand. And with the right text..." She pulled out the pen she kept in her purse for autographs, clicked it on, and wrote:

> *Michelle,*
> *as long as I have you, I don't need Cupid. Will you be my Valentine?*

There. Short and sweet. She signed the card, "love, Amanda," and then, as an afterthought, added another line.

> *P.S. Yes. It's a date.*

ABOUT JAE

Jae grew up amidst the vineyards of southern Germany. She spent her childhood with her nose buried in a book, earning her the nickname "professor." The writing bug bit her at the age of eleven. For the last eight years, she has been writing mostly in English.

She used to work as a psychologist but gave up her day job in December 2013 to become a full-time writer and a part-time editor. As far as she's concerned, it's the best job in the world.

When she's not writing, she likes to spend her time reading, indulging her ice cream and office supply addictions, and watching way too many crime shows.

CONNECT WITH JAE ONLINE

Jae loves hearing from readers!

E-mail her at: jae@jae-fiction.com
Visit her website: jae-fiction.com
Visit her blog: jae-fiction.com/blog
Like her on Facebook: facebook.com/JaeAuthor
Follow her on Twitter: @jaefiction

EXCERPT FROM
SOMETHING IN THE WINE

BY JAE

FLINCHING, DREW SPAT OUT THE sip of wine she'd just taken and frowned at the glass. *Ugh! What's this? Wine or vinegar?* She shook herself. *Buying the cheap stuff again, Jake, my friend?* She craned her neck, searching for a member of the catering staff weaving around the party guests. *Ah, there.*

A woman in black slacks and a white blouse gathered empty and abandoned glasses from the bar.

Drew headed toward her to get rid of the swill masquerading as wine. When the woman turned around with a tray full of glasses, Drew's steps faltered. She stopped a few yards away. *Oh, wow. She's cute.* Still watching the woman, she moved closer.

The server wasn't the type of stunning beauty Drew was usually attracted to, but something about her captured her attention. Maybe it was the strange mix of strength and vulnerability in the woman's features and her posture.

She moved like a mouse—quietly, but efficiently, as if she didn't want to draw anyone's attention.

Even from a few steps away, Drew could tell that the woman was tall, but despite her height, she didn't appear imposing. Her gaze was too shy for that. A cute nose and the gentle curve of her lips contrasted with a stubborn chin. Golden hair—the color of a fine, mature white wine—brushed against her slender shoulders. The woman took a hand off the tray to sweep an unruly strand behind her ear.

The tray tilted to one side.

Drew set down her glass and jumped forward in full knight-in-shining-armor mode to rescue the tray and the damsel in distress. She reached out just as the woman realized what was happening and straightened the tray.

Unable to stop her forward momentum, Drew collided with the tray, which catapulted one of the half-filled glasses through the air.

Cold liquid hit her in the chest. Reflexively, she caught the now empty glass before it could fall to the floor and shatter.

She froze. So did the woman.

Wide green eyes stared down at her from behind horn-rimmed glasses.

Drew realized that her damsel was at least four or five inches taller than her own five foot six.

"Oh, my God! I'm so sorry!" With trembling fingers, the woman balanced the tray in one hand and picked up a napkin.

For a moment, Drew imagined the woman's hands on her, dabbing at her drenched shirt, but instead, the woman handed her the napkin. She tried to soak up the worst of the spill but realized her shirt was ruined. *Guess I'm more of a knight in wine-stained armor now.*

"Are you okay?" the woman asked.

"I'm fine. No harm done." Drew wiped a drop of red wine off her chin. "Well, almost none."

A blush crept up the woman's slender neck and brought color to her cheeks. "I'll pay for the dry cleaning, of course."

Drew smiled. *How cute.* She couldn't remember ever seeing any of her worldly, confident girlfriends blush, which lent a hint of vulnerability that softened the stranger's earnest features. "Don't worry about it."

Laughter from the people around them made Drew tear her gaze away from the woman.

A few of Jake's friends pointed out Drew's stained shirt to one another and seemed to find it hysterically funny.

The woman's cheeks went from pink to a dark rosé.

The swift surge of protectiveness rising in her chest surprised Drew. She made eye contact with the worst offenders. "What?" She pulled the wet shirt away from her skin and grinned. "Haven't you ever seen a woman wearing a glass of wine? It's all the rage, really."

A few of the guests laughed and finally directed their gazes away from Drew and her damsel.

"Your shirt looks expensive," the blonde woman said. "I could pay for—"

"No, you don't need to do that. I was the one who hit the tray, so if anyone needs to apologize, it's me. I saw the glasses sliding to the edge of the tray and thought I could help, but instead I gave you quite a scare, plowing into you like that." She gasped, only then realizing she hadn't taken a breath between sentences. "I'm really sorry. Maybe I could invite you for coffee to make up for it." She had casually asked out many women in her life, but now she found herself rambling.

The woman glanced at her. Drew thought she saw puzzlement in her eyes, which, at this distance, were the color of vine leaves in spring. Then the woman frowned and shook her head. "And risk spilling hot beverages on you too? Better not."

When the woman moved to walk around her, Drew quickly stepped forward and blocked her way, not ready to give up yet. "That's a risk worth taking. So, how about it? Will you have coffee with me?"

"It's nice of you to offer, but it's not necessary. It was just an accident, and I really need to go now." The woman turned her wrist to glance at her watch, making the tray tilt again.

Ignoring the possibility of further damage to her clothes, Drew grabbed for the tray. Her fingers wrapped around the woman's, her tanned hands contrasting sharply with the ivory of the woman's skin.

"Sorry." Another blush stained the woman's cheeks. "I'm not usually such a klutz."

"Don't worry about it." Drew relinquished her hold on the tray, but not without letting her index finger linger against the woman's hand for a moment. "Being a bit clumsy has a certain charm," she said with a wink.

The woman lifted an eyebrow but didn't return the flirtatious smile.

Damn, she's straight. Drew suppressed a sigh.

"I need to go," the woman said. "Again, I'm sorry. Maybe you can borrow one of Jake's shirts for the evening."

She's on a first-name basis with Jake? For a moment, Drew wondered whether the blonde was one of Jake's many lovers, but then she shook her head. With her horn-rimmed glasses, stubborn chin, and make-up-free face, this woman wasn't Jake's type.

She glanced down at the wet shirt plastered against her full breasts. "I'm afraid Jake and I are not quite the same...um...size."

The woman blushed for the fourth time, and Drew caught her glancing at her chest.

Maybe she's not so straight after all. Drew grinned and decided to help her cover the awkward silence. "It's okay. I was just about to go say hello to Jake and then head home anyway." She nodded toward the tray. "You need any help with that?"

"No, thanks, I can manage."

"All right." Drew was running out of reasons to keep talking for a while longer, so she reluctantly stepped out of the way.

Her damsel said good-bye and walked away.

Drew stood watching the gentle sway of her hips. *Nice.* She pinched the wet shirt between two fingers and pulled it away from her skin. After a final glance at the stranger, she went in search of Jake.

"What the hell happened to you?" Jake asked when she found him. "I go to the bathroom for a minute, and when I come back, you look like a murder victim."

Drew glanced at her wine-drenched shirt and shrugged. "I met a woman."

A teasing grin formed on Jake's lips. "Don't they normally wait until after dessert to throw their drinks at you?"

"They? One woman, okay? It was just one woman who threw her drink at me, and that was ages ago."

"And you deserved it. Dude, you were a dog back in the day!"

Not those old war stories again! Okay, she had dated a lot of women in college, but she had left that part of her life behind when she had taken over her family's vineyard. "That was in college, and you slept with more women in a week than I did during my entire freshman year!"

"Yeah, the good ol' times." Jake's dreamy sigh ruffled the shaggy blond hair falling into his face. "So, what have you been up to? I haven't seen you since the AIDS fundraiser we did at the gym. And that was what? Two months ago?"

"Three," Drew said. "I just finished bringing in my first harvest. I've been out in the vineyards every day since we started harvesting the grapes for the sparkling wines back in August." She rubbed her eyes. The past weeks had left her exhausted but also filled with a sense of accomplishment. She hoped her parents would have been proud of her.

"Ah, work, work, work." Jake wagged his finger at her. "You're beginning to remind me of my sister."

When they had gone to college together, Drew had heard stories about Jake's sister, Annie—or rather about the practical jokes Jake had played on her when they'd been children. She had never met her, though. "Are you ever going to introduce me to your mysterious sister?"

"I would have introduced you years ago, but convincing Annie to come to one of my parties is harder than getting an audience with the pope."

Good for her. Drew bit back a grin.

"And you," Jake slapped her shoulder, "never had the time in all these years to meet my folks during spring break."

Drew hit him back, but her slap bounced off the wiry muscles he had developed as a climber. "Yeah, because I had to help in the vineyard while you, the slacker, partied the whole time."

"Okay, okay, I'll introduce you. I saw her talking to Rob earlier, so she has to be around here somewhere." Jake turned and looked around, then pivoted to face Drew. "But remember: no flirting. She's straight."

Drew lifted her hands. "I'm not interested in your baby sister. In fact, I just saw a woman at the buffet. For some reason, she really caught my attention. I think she's working for the catering service."

"The brunette with the killer legs?"

"No. This one is a blonde, and if her legs kill you, it's probably because she's a bit clumsy." At the memory of the woman almost dropping the tray of glasses a second time, Drew had to smile.

A frown carved a deep line between Jake's brows. "I don't think I hired a blonde."

"Yes, you did. She knows you by name."

"The only clumsy blonde I know at this party is…" Jake paused and laughed. "Is she tall, green-eyed, and serious as a heart attack?"

Drew suppressed the urge to defend her clumsy damsel. "Sounds about right." Belatedly, she realized she had never found out the woman's name.

"Ah, that blonde."

"So you do know her?" Drew asked. "Could you introduce us?"

"Sure, no problem." A sound almost like a giggle escaped Jake's mouth.

Someone should tell him that straight men don't giggle. But for now, Drew was more interested in finding out more about the woman. "Do you know if she's family?"

The giggles turned into a belly laugh. Jake slapped his thighs, nearly spilling his drink all over himself. "Oh, yeah. She's family."

"Really? She is?" When the woman hadn't flirted back and hadn't even seemed to notice her interest, she had given up hope. "Are you sure?"

"One hundred percent," Jake said, still grinning madly.

"And she's single?"

Jake rolled his eyes. "Has been for ages."

Drew couldn't believe her good fortune. "Sounds like you've known her for a long time."

"Yeah, you could say that." Jake turned. "Wait here. I'll go get her."

Something in the Wine is available as a paperback and in various e-book formats at many online bookstores.

OTHER BOOKS FROM
YLVA PUBLISHING

http://www.ylva-publishing.com

SOMETHING IN THE WINE

JAE

ISBN: 978-3-95533-005-7

Length: 393 pages

All her life, Annie Prideaux has suffered through her brother's constant practical jokes only he thinks are funny. But Jake's last joke is one too many, she decides when he sets her up on a blind date with his friend Drew Corbin— neglecting to tell his straight sister one tiny detail: her date is not a man, but a lesbian.

Annie and Drew decide it's time to turn the tables on Jake by pretending to fall in love with each other.

At first glance, they have nothing in common. Disillusioned with love, Annie focuses on books, her cat, and her work as an accountant while Drew, more confident and outgoing, owns a dog and spends most of her time working in her beloved vineyard.

Only their common goal to take revenge on Jake unites them. But what starts as a table-turning game soon turns Annie's and Drew's lives upside down as the lines between pretending and reality begin to blur.

Something in the Wine is a story about love, friendship, and coming to terms with what it means to be yourself.

CONFLICT OF INTEREST
(revised edition)

JAE
ISBN: 978-3-95533-109-2
Length: 467 pages

Workaholic Detective Aiden Carlisle isn't looking for love—and certainly not at the law enforcement seminar she reluctantly agreed to attend. But the first lecturer is not at all what she expected.

Psychologist Dawn Kinsley has just found her place in life. After a failed relationship with a police officer, she has sworn never to get involved with another cop again, but she feels a connection to Aiden from the very first moment.

Can Aiden keep from crossing the line when a brutal crime threatens to keep them apart before they've even gotten together?

HEARTS AND FLOWERS BORDER
(revised edition)

L.T. SMITH
ISBN: 978-3-95533-179-5
Length: 291 pages

A visitor from her past jolts Laura Stewart into memories—some funny, some heart-wrenching. Thirteen years ago, Laura buried those memories so deeply she never believed they would resurface. Still, the pain of first love mars Laura's present life and might even destroy her chance of happiness with the beautiful, yet seemingly unobtainable Emma Jenkins.

Can Laura let go of the past, or will she make the same mistakes all over again?

Hearts and Flowers Border is a simple tale of the uncertainty of youth and the first flush of love—love that may have a chance after all.

COMING HOME
(revised edition)

LOIS CLOAREC HART
ISBN: 978-3-95533-064-4
Length: 371 pages

A triangle with a twist, *Coming Home* is the story of three good people caught up in an impossible situation.

Rob, a charismatic ex-fighter pilot severely disabled with MS, has been steadfastly cared for by his wife, Jan, for many years. Quite by accident one day, Terry, a young writer/postal carrier, enters their lives and turns it upside down.

Injecting joy and turbulence into their quiet existence, Terry draws Rob and Jan into her lively circle of family and friends until the growing attachment between the two women begins to strain the bonds of love and loyalty, to Rob and each other.

IN A HEARTBEAT

RJ NOLAN
ISBN: 978-3-95533-159-7
Length: 370 pages

Veteran police officer Sam McKenna has no trouble facing down criminals on a daily basis but breaks out in a sweat at the mere mention of commitment. A recent failed relationship strengthens her resolve to stick with her trademark no-strings-attached affairs.

Dr. Riley Connolly, a successful trauma surgeon, has spent her whole life trying to measure up to her family's expectations. And that includes hiding her sexuality from them.

When a routine call sends Sam to the hospital where Riley works, the two women are hurtled into a life-and-death situation. The incident binds them together. But can there be any future for a commitment-phobic cop and a closeted, workaholic doctor?

COMING FROM YLVA
PUBLISHING IN FALL 2014

http://www.ylva-publishing.com

STILL LIFE

L.T. SMITH

After breaking off her relationship with a female lothario, Jess Taylor decides she doesn't want to expose herself to another cheating partner. Staying at home, alone, suits her just fine. Her idea of a good night is an early one—preferably with a good book. Well, until her best friend, Sophie Harrison, decides it's time Jess rejoined the human race.

Trying to pull Jess from her self-imposed prison, Sophie signs them both up for a Still Life art class at the local college. Sophie knows the beautiful art teacher, Diana Sullivan, could be the woman her best friend needs to move on with her life.

But, in reality, could art bring these two women together? Could it be strong enough to make a masterpiece in just twelve sessions? And, more importantly, can Jess overcome her fear of being used once again?

Only time will tell.

BARRING COMPLICATIONS

BLYTHE RIPPON

It's an open secret that the newest justice on the Supreme Court is a lesbian. So when the Court decides to hear a case about gay marriage, Justice Victoria Willoughby must navigate the press, sway at least one of her conservative colleagues, and confront her own fraught feelings about coming out.

Just when she decides she's up to the challenge, she learns that the very brilliant, very out Genevieve Fornier will be lead counsel on the case.

Genevieve isn't sure which is causing her more sleepless nights: the prospect of losing the case, or the thought of who will be sitting on the bench when she argues it.

Departure from the Script
© by Jae

ISBN: 978-3-95533-195-5

Also available as e-book.

Published by Ylva Publishing, legal entity of Ylva Verlag, e.Kfr.

Ylva Verlag, e.Kfr.
Owner: Astrid Ohletz
Am Kirschgarten 2
65830 Kriftel
Germany

http://www.ylva-publishing.com

First edition: July 2014

Credits
Edited by Judy Underwood and Nikki Busch
Cover Design by Streetlight Graphics

Lightning Source UK Ltd.
Milton Keynes UK
UKOW04f1901200215

246664UK00001B/24/P